THE INN ON HANGING HILL

THE BEACH HOUSE MYSTERY SERIES

CHRISTY BARRITT

River Heights

"WE SHOULDN'T BE DOING THIS," Lindsey Waters whispered as she stood in the dark hallway next to her sometimes friend, sometimes enemy, and all-the-time troublemaker.

"This is our only chance to see the water glowing."

She stared up into Benjamin's dancing gaze and frowned. "Are you sure?"

"I heard one of the guests talking about how this is a once-in-a-lifetime opportunity. Don't you want to see it yourself?"

Lindsey nibbled on her bottom lip before nodding. She did want to see it, but she hated making her parents mad. "If we're caught, my mom is going to kill me. She won't let us hang out together anymore."

"Then we can't get caught." Benjamin offered a rakish grin, his mussed honey-blond hair and dimples making him look trustworthy. "Now, let's do this."

They gripped their flashlights as they headed down the hall on the first floor of the Hidden Shores Inn, which Lindsey's family owned.

The place was old—and it smelled old. It stood two stories high with balconies across the backside of the building. Benjamin's father had worked as a caretaker here for the past two years.

Everyone else—staff and guests—were sleeping. If Lindsey and Benjamin woke anyone up, they'd be in trouble. Lindsey's mom didn't play games, especially when it came to business. *Every guest deserves an incredible experience they'll want to tell their friends about. That's how you grow a business.* That's what her mom always said.

Lindsey hardly ever disobeyed her stern mother. But Eleanor Waters had been especially uptight lately, and nothing Lindsey did could make her mom happy. She'd missed a corner while vacuuming, the dishes she washed weren't spotless, and there was a wrinkle after she made her bed.

Benjamin placed his finger over his mouth as he nodded toward the back door.

As soon as they were outside, the wind and waves would obscure any other sounds from their late-night adventure.

In theory, at least.

It was past midnight. No one else should be awake.

But were they?

As Lindsey stepped onto the sprawling deck facing the Chesapeake Bay, she nearly stumbled over a trunk.

A trunk? What was that doing here? Who had left it?

She stared at the large, leather-covered piece.

She'd figure out where it had come from later. Maybe she would even open it and see what was inside. Most likely, it just held blankets or quilts.

Benjamin pointed to the water. "Can you see it?"

Lindsey sucked in a breath as she glanced at the waves.

Sure enough, there it was.

Bioluminescence.

She'd read about it in one of her books during science class. But Lindsey couldn't believe she was seeing it with her own eyes.

"Let's get closer," Benjamin said.

They trotted down the wooden steps leading to the cliff overlooking the Chesapeake Bay.

Still gripping their flashlights, they reached a second set of stairs and began walking down the bluff toward the water.

As they stepped to the sandy beach below, they crept closer to the waves. Lindsey sucked in a breath. The water looked magical, almost like fairies lived in the waves.

Fairies . . . if she made a wish, would the fairies grant her request? Maybe they'd carry her away from this place and take her somewhere happy. Was that asking too much?

Benjamin reached over and squeezed her hand.

Just in a friendly gesture. Lindsey was only twelve, and Benjamin was fourteen. They were too young to date. Not that she would want to date Benjamin. He was like a brother—a brother who liked to get her in trouble.

She continued to stare at the water. "This is the most beautiful thing I've ever seen in my whole life."

The waves glowed a neon blue-green.

Algae caused the phenomenon. That's what she'd read.

But Lindsey never thought she'd get to see it for herself.

"I want to do stuff like this for the rest of my life," Benjamin said.

"Stuff like what?"

"New adventures. See new places. Experience new things."

"You want to do that always?"

He nodded. "Always. Settling down sounds boring, doesn't it?"

"Not to me. I just want to be in a place that makes me happy with people who make me feel safe."

"Do I make you feel safe?" Benjamin turned toward her.

When she heard the earnestness in his voice, she licked her lips. The truth was: no, he didn't. Benjamin was too much of a wildcard. But since they were only a couple of years apart and both the only children in their families, they spent a lot of time together. In other circumstances, she couldn't see them being friends.

Instead of answering, she changed the subject. "We should get back before somebody notices we're gone."

"Let's go."

As they neared the top of the steps that stretched up the cliff, a shadow moved in the distance.

Lindsey froze and grabbed Benjamin's arm. "Did you see that?"

He glanced around. "See what?"

"Someone is outside the inn." Fear cracked her voice. "Walking around."

Benjamin tensed before shrugging and letting out a breath. "It's probably the moon and the shadows and the wind. Nobody should be out right now."

Lindsey nibbled on her bottom lip a moment before nodding.

Benjamin had good instincts. He was probably right. Besides, why would anyone be awake at this time of the night?

They reached the top of the cliff and hurried toward the inn. As they did, Lindsey's gaze wandered to the area she'd seen that shadow. A blurred image came into view, and she swallowed back a scream.

Benjamin turned to her with his worried gaze. "What is it, Lindsey?"

She couldn't speak. Instead, she raised her hand and pointed to a massive oak tree that stood on the edge of the property. The one she'd played under as a child. The one that had once held a tire swing and where Benjamin had carved their initials.

"Stay here." Benjamin stepped away, almost as if he wanted to check it out himself.

That seemed like a terrible idea. A really terrible idea.

As the wind shifted, so did the shadow.

Someone was definitely there.

Hanging by a rope from one of the branches.

Dead.

Lindsey was certain of it.

A scream rose in her throat again. Before she could unleash it, a hand slapped across her mouth.

"Lindsey!" Benjamin charged back toward her, his normally carefree gaze filled with worry.

But before he reached her, something came down over her head. Something dark. Hooded. Its musty smell made it hard to breathe.

"You're not supposed to be out here," someone whispered.

Then everything went black.

CHAPTER ONE

PRESENT DAY

AS LINDSEY WATERS stepped into the old inn, dust and memories stirred around her.

No one had been in the place in nearly fourteen years.

Including Lindsey.

She never thought she'd come back. But she needed closure and a change of environment, so here she was.

Hidden Shores Inn. The place where she'd grown up. Her childhood home, with all the good and bad memories that came with it.

Lindsey had tried to leave it behind, but the task was impossible. The memories always stayed with her, even when she didn't want them to.

Except sometimes she longed for the memories.

Memories of what had happened to her during the two weeks she'd been missing.

But no one knew or, if they did, they kept it a secret, and her recollections had never resurfaced.

Lindsey swallowed so hard her throat ached.

She left the door open behind her as she stepped deeper into the space. She flicked on the light switch, but the bulbs on a chandelier in the center of the foyer remained dark.

The power company had told her it could take a couple of days to get the electricity turned on, but she'd been hoping it would be sooner rather than later.

As she stepped farther inside, images of the fancy guests who'd once adorned this space filled her mind. There had been eighteen rooms people could reserve as they tried to "get away from it all" here at Hidden Shores. That was what her mother had always said.

Then even stronger images emerged. The ones of Lindsey with a blanket draped over her shoulders being brought back to this place by Sheriff Ross after she'd been found in the nearby woods. A hushed, almost stunned air had surrounded her, as if she'd been brought back from the dead.

Her gut clenched, and she shoved those memories aside.

All she needed was to get this place in shape and then she'd put the historic inn on the market. She'd tried to hire a general contractor to do the work, but good help was apparently hard to find. Plus, she'd been told by multiple people that she didn't understand the scope of the work.

Clearly, they were right.

This place was a dump. A water stain stared at her from the ceiling, the shape of it reminding her of an eyeball. Wallpaper peeled from the walls. The drapes in the distance were faded and falling from the crooked rod tasked with keeping them straight.

Lindsey reached for her necklace and squeezed the keys there.

Skeleton keys.

She'd begun collecting them when she was sixteen. She loved nothing more than scouring antique shops looking for new pieces to add to her collection. Her favorites made it onto this long gold chain she often wore.

She liked to think about what these keys would unlock. How they may have been precious to somebody at one time.

In some ways, the keys signified her past and the memories that remained locked away.

She let out a breath. There was no time to waste here. She had to make a list of what needed to be done and find somebody to help her.

Then she'd be gone. Out of here. Away from this place and the pain it brought back.

She walked through the foyer, into the dining room, and then through the swinging double doors into the kitchen.

Buying groceries and preparing a place to sleep would be her first priority. Then she'd worry about everything else.

She'd been tempted to get a hotel in town instead of staying in this dusty old place. But then people might start talking and asking questions she had no desire to answer.

She and her parents had lived on the first floor near the kitchen. Three full-time employees had also lived there, including Benjamin and his father for two years.

Lindsey pushed through a second doorway in the kitchen, one leading to the staff quarters. As she started down the hallway, the wooden floor beneath her creaked just as it had done when she was a child.

She passed three doors until pausing by her childhood bedroom.

Her hand gripped the handle, and she started to

twist it when she paused.

As her skin prickled, she turned and glanced down the hallway.

A shadowed figure stood there.

She let out a gasp and jumped back.

Who was here? And what did he want?

BENJAMIN PAUSED at the start of the hallway and sucked in a breath.

Lindsey.

She was here.

She'd arrived earlier than he'd expected.

"I didn't mean to scare you," he started. "The gate was open, and the front door unlocked. I knocked, but you must not have heard me."

She continued to stare.

Benjamin stepped closer, emerging from the shadows so she could see his face. A small window at the end of the hallway allowed a beam of autumn sunlight to fill the space.

"It's just me," he told her.

Lindsey backed against the wall, her hand clutching her heart. But as his face came into view, her expression morphed from fearful to curious.

"Who are you?" The slight tremble in her voice gave away her fear.

His pulse sped as he realized this was a pivotal moment. "You really don't recognize me?"

She continued to stare, not saying anything. Her eyes flickered back and forth with thought. He could almost see her thoughts racing, formulating, searching.

"It's me," he offered quietly.

Lindsey squinted before letting out a gasp. "Benjamin?"

His heart continued to thrum as he forced out a chuckle. "The one and only."

She stepped closer, still appearing shocked with her tight expression and narrowed eyes. "Benjamin Newsom? You look . . . different."

He shrugged and raised his hands. "What can I say? I grew up."

"Yes, you did." As she reached forward and offered a quick hug, the aroma of vanilla-scented shampoo filled his nostrils. "I can't believe it's you. What are you doing here?"

"I heard you were looking for a handyman."

"You're a handyman?" Surprise laced her voice as she stepped back, her expression still optimistically cautious.

He shrugged again. "My dad taught me a few things, I guess."

"But . . . you don't live around here anymore . . . do you?"

"I don't. But I'd planned on heading back here anyway for a long overdue visit. Then I heard you were looking for someone to fix up this place. I saw the ad you took out in the online newspaper. I actually texted you about it."

"But you never mentioned your name."

"I thought I might surprise you. I wasn't sure if telling you my name would be a help or a hinderance . . ."

"I still can't believe this . . ." Disbelief stretched through her airy voice.

He grinned. "I'd say. You look really good, Lindsey."

She glanced down at the faded jeans and T-shirt she wore. "Yes, really good. Clearly."

His grin widened. Lindsey was a natural beauty. Benjamin had seen her social media pictures. Kept up with her life in that regard. She always looked good, even without trying.

"It's been . . . fifteen years," she murmured. "I didn't think you'd want to speak with me again."

"I know what you're thinking. I don't blame you

for anything that happened." His voice tightened at the tragic events of that time period. He'd wondered how Lindsey had handled it over the years.

Lindsey stepped back. "You should blame me. Especially after what happened to your dad—"

He shushed her. "Let's not talk about that. Not yet. Okay?"

Tears flooded her gaze as she nodded a little too erratically. "Okay. Okay then. Yes." She wiped beneath her eyes and drew in a shaky breath "You're really here to help?"

"Only if you'll hire me."

She extended her hand as if ready to seal the deal. "As long as you don't get me in trouble like you used to when we were kids, you're hired."

He stared at her hand a moment before shaking it. Her quick response surprised him. "I'll do my best to keep you out of trouble. How does that sound?"

"That sounds perfect." Her smile faded as she glanced around. "Truthfully, no one else wants to touch this place."

He glanced around at the rotting wood and years of neglect. "I can't imagine why."

"As I'm sure you remember, locals think it's haunted. Even more so in recent years."

"I can't blame them after . . ." Now why had he

brought that up?

Lindsey rubbed her throat. "Exactly." She drew in a deep breath as if pulling herself together. "I just can't get over the fact that you're here. Have I said that yet?"

He grinned. "Maybe once or twice."

"And you've grown into such a man."

He shrugged. "It was bound to happen."

She let out a shaky laugh. "Listen to me rambling on. Let me grab my stuff. I need to run to the store to get a few things and then get a room ready to sleep in for the night. I'd love to catch up with you later, though."

"Whatever you need. I'm here to help, not to cause you more stress."

She smiled at him again. But her eyes . . . they were almost haunted yet so innocent at the same time.

But *was* she innocent? Was she really?

The sincerity in her gaze caused guilt to flood him.

What would Lindsey think when she found out his ulterior motives?

Suddenly, coming here felt like a bad idea.

He had thought he fit this job description . . . but what if he was wrong?

CHAPTER TWO

LINDSEY COULDN'T BELIEVE Benjamin was here after all these years. She never thought she'd see him again.

In some ways, he looked the same, yet in other regards he seemed so different.

He still had that mussed honey-blond hair. A burly, muscular build. Haunted green eyes.

He'd definitely grown into a man—a very handsome man with broad shoulders, a stubble-like beard, and a gaze hinting at years of life experiences.

And he was here.

That realization still blew Lindsey's mind.

"Where are you staying while you're in town?" She shifted as they stood in the hallway.

"I'm trying to find a room at a local hotel. They're

all a good twenty minutes away from here, but I don't think that will be a problem."

The thought seemed ridiculous. Besides, it would be nice to have someone close by. Lindsey had dreaded staying in this huge place by herself. On a more practical level, Benjamin wouldn't have to waste time traveling here to work either.

"Why don't you just stay in one of the extra rooms here?" she offered. "Certainly, there's got to be a couple that are habitable."

Benjamin rubbed his jaw as if the idea made him uncomfortable. "I don't want to impose."

"Don't be ridiculous. Besides, if you stay here not only will it be easier to work, but it will give us a chance to catch up. It's been a long time." Her throat tightened as she said the words. It wasn't all happy memories between them.

"Yes, it has been a long time." Benjamin's voice sounded mellow with remorse.

Lindsey couldn't blame him. So much had happened. So much tragedy. This inn seemed to embody it all.

They paused as they walked toward the front door.

"How about if we run to get some groceries and

then we can come back here and nail down a plan for this place?" she suggested.

"As much as I would love to head to the store with you, I have a better idea. Why don't we divide and conquer? I'll get a couple of rooms ready and, while I do that, you could buy the groceries." He glanced at his watch. "It's already past three. We only have a few hours of daylight left."

"Sounds like a plan."

"Great." He nodded toward the rooms in the distance. "I'll get started then and see what I can do here before it gets dark. It doesn't look like the power company has turned on the electricity yet. I brought a generator with me, just in case."

"Smart thinking. And, hopefully, it should be on by tomorrow." Lindsey stared at him another moment, still in disbelief that he was actually here. "Okay. That sounds wonderful. Thank you. You're a real godsend."

"I don't know about that." His gaze clouded for a moment.

Lindsey paused. Why did Benjamin look out of sorts? Was it something she'd said?

She didn't know, but she'd have to worry about that later.

As Lindsey grabbed her purse and stepped

toward the door, she wondered if coming here truly would bring the closure—and reprieve from her problems—that she needed.

BENJAMIN COULDN'T STOP his thoughts from racing as he cleaned up an old spare bedroom as well as Lindsey's. Thankfully, all the furniture had been left when this place was abandoned fourteen years ago.

As he worked, Lindsey's image fluttered through his mind.

Lindsey . . . she was far more beautiful than he'd thought she would be. A smattering of freckles colored her cheeks. Her straight blonde hair fell to her shoulders. Her greenish-blue eyes appeared kind but cautious.

Her abduction and the fallout from it had done a number on her, hadn't it? Just what else had these past few years held for her?

He didn't know the answers. With any luck, maybe she'd open up.

For now, he opened the windows. The gentle, sixty-five-degree breeze brought a welcome burst of freshness inside the stale space. He beat some old quilts outside, trying to rid them of years of neglect. He found a duster and quickly demolished any spiderwebs and dust balls.

Thankfully, Lindsey had called in advance to get the water turned on. That would make their stay here a lot easier.

But this would be a big job.

Not just fixing up this inn, but everything else that needed to be done also.

Benjamin paused and leaned against the window for a moment, staring out at the Chesapeake Bay as it glimmered in the fading sunlight.

What a beautiful sight.

So different from the mountains he'd looked at out his window in Tennessee. He'd thought they were the most beautiful thing a person could see. But, being here again, he knew he was wrong.

Tension pulled tight across his chest.

Was he really up for this job?

Truthfully, he didn't know. He wanted to say that he was. He desperately needed the money. Not for himself, but for Natalie.

This was all for a good cause, he reminded himself. He had to keep that at the forefront of his mind.

Justice needed to be served.

As he heard the front door open, he rushed to help Lindsey. Her arms were loaded with groceries as she teetered inside.

"Let me help you." He took two bags from her and walked toward the kitchen.

"Thanks," she muttered behind him. "I have a couple more bags to grab."

A few minutes later, they were both in the kitchen unloading the groceries under the light of a few LED lanterns that had been set up. Lindsey had also bought some ice. Until Benjamin got the generator working, they would need to use coolers to keep things refrigerated. It wasn't ideal, but the fix should work, at least temporarily.

"You got a tattoo." Lindsey pointed to his forearm.

He glanced at the image of the Lion of Judah before quickly pulling down his sleeve. "I did."

"You used to always say you'd never get a tattoo, that your grandma would disown you if you did."

He shrugged, hoping Lindsey couldn't see his flushed cheeks. "What can I say? People grow up. People change."

"I guess that they do." Her smile faded as she leaned against the kitchen counter. "I know that people always say that life comes full circle. But in all the years since I left this place, I never thought the day would come when you and I would both be here again."

"I understand." His voice sounded hoarse as the words left his mouth. "There are a lot of emotions that go along with this, aren't there?"

"Yes, there are." She glanced out the window. "At least the sunsets are just as beautiful as ever."

"No one can argue that."

She grabbed a bag of chips and set them on the counter, the crinkling sound of the package filling the air.

As she turned to him, Benjamin braced himself for whatever she might have to say.

But before any words left her lips, a creak sounded above them.

They both froze.

Lindsey's gaze met his, and questions floated between them.

They'd both heard the sound. That was for sure.

Then another creak sounded and another.

Benjamin knew exactly what that was.

Footsteps.

Someone else was in the inn.

CHAPTER THREE

BENJAMIN HEARD the footsteps above him.

Why would someone be in this old place? Was it a squatter?

He'd intended to arrive early to check out the place before Lindsey got here. But he hadn't had the chance. He'd arrived just a little too late. That traffic accident he passed on the way had delayed him more than he thought.

He grabbed a hammer from the toolchest he'd brought in from his truck and stepped forward. "I'm going to go check it out."

"You don't have to," Lindsey rushed. "We can call the police."

"Whoever's up there could be gone by time they

could get here. I need to see what's going on. Especially if we're going to sleep here tonight."

She stared at him with wide eyes but finally nodded. "Be careful. Please." Her voice quivered as if fear was starting to consume her.

The reaction had come on quickly enough that it surprised him.

As he heard the floor creak again, Benjamin knew he couldn't waste any more time. "Go to your room. Lock your door. And if anything happens, call the police."

Lindsey nodded, almost looking dazed.

With one last glance at her, he started toward the rickety stairway in the main entry.

It was dark. He should have grabbed a flashlight. But he hadn't been thinking, only reacting.

Quietly, he crept up the stairs, testing each board to make sure he wouldn't fall through.

He was definitely going to have his work cut out for him here. But that was something to worry about at another time.

He continued upward until he reached the landing at the top. Then he turned to the hallway on the left. That's where the sound came from.

If he remembered this place well enough, there

were six rooms down this hallway where guests had stayed back when this inn was operational.

The footsteps could have come from any of them.

A bad feeling continued to grow in his gut.

Slowly, he crept toward the entryway. Both the north and south wings had doors at their upstairs entrances, mostly for privacy and sound-control purposes he assumed.

Using his foot, he nudged the door open.

A dark hallway stared back. A hallway full of possibilities. Deadly possibilities.

Someone could be hiding behind any of those doorways, waiting to strike.

Had someone broken into the inn to steal something? To hurt someone? Perhaps it was just someone being nosy.

Or Benjamin's original theory could be correct. Maybe a squatter had been using this old place.

If that was the case, Benjamin would think he'd have seen some type of evidence in the kitchen. But there had been no signs of anyone living here.

He shoved the questions aside. Right now, he needed to put all his focus and energy on staying alert and figuring out who else was wandering this inn.

As he stepped into the hallway, his eyes slowly adjusted to the darkness. Without any windows, the air was mostly an inky blob in front of him.

He crept forward until he reached the first door. Cautiously, he twisted the knob and opened it.

Still holding the handle, he peered inside. He saw nothing. But that didn't mean that no one was hiding somewhere in the dark recesses of the room.

He stepped further inside. As he did, he grabbed his phone and opened the flashlight app. He swung the light around the room, dust captured in the beam.

This whole inn was eerie, the perfect place for a ghost story. The old building had all the right elements in place, including a sordid history. In fact, the area where the inn was located had originally been called Hanging Hill by locals because of some tragedies that occurred here more than a century ago.

Benjamin walked past an antique dresser covered in dust. A gilded mirror. A four-poster bed with turned wooden corners and a moth-eaten quilt atop it.

He stepped around the bed and shone his light on the other side to make sure no one was hiding there.

He held his breath with anticipation.

But the space was empty.

Quickly, he moved across the room again and opened the door to the bathroom. The hinges let out an eerie creak that sent a shiver up his spine.

He wasn't normally the type to get easily spooked. But if any place could do it, this one could.

One room down, and only five more to go.

He supposed that thought should bring him some comfort, but it didn't.

Just as he stepped out into the hallway, he heard a *whoosh* beside him.

He hardly had time to look up before someone rammed into him. He staggered into the dresser just inside the bedroom doorway, bruising his ribs against the furniture as he fell to the floor and hit his head.

Footsteps pounded away.

Benjamin quickly pulled himself to his feet, determined to catch this guy.

LINDSEY REMAINED in the bedroom with the door locked, just as she'd promised. But she couldn't stop thinking about what was going on upstairs.

Footsteps sounded. Was that one set or two?

She pressed her eyes closed. One, she hoped.

Please, Lord, watch over Benjamin.

She pressed herself into the corner, still waiting. She hated doing nothing. However, she'd promised Benjamin she would stay.

But what if he needed her? What if he was hurt right now?

At that thought, she stepped forward. She hadn't reached the door when she heard a crash. Her back muscles tightened.

She quickened her steps, unlocked the door, and threw it open. Peering down the hallway, she searched for a sign of anyone. But there was no one. Just an unnerving silence.

Until she heard the footsteps again.

The stairs. Those footsteps were thundering down the stairs.

She always remembered the sound of footsteps on the grand stairway. Her dad had been a big man who'd stomped wherever he went. Her mom had always been on his case about it.

Lindsey glanced around, knowing she needed something to defend herself with, just in case there was trouble.

The only thing she could find was an old candle-stick. It seemed cliché, but she grabbed it anyway. The brass decoration was heavy. She was surprised that after all these years of this place being uninhab-ited everything remotely valuable hadn't been stolen.

But maybe in a small town like this, such crimes didn't happen.

Lindsey knew that wasn't true. Horrible things could happen in small towns. She was living proof of it.

Gripping the candlestick like a baseball bat, she crept forward. Before she even reached the end of the hallway, a door opened and then slammed.

The front door, she realized. Someone had just gone outside.

Lindsey quickened her steps.

Just as she stepped into the foyer, she spotted Benjamin hurrying down the staircase. He barely gave her a glance as he rushed toward the door.

As she hurried to catch up with him, he yanked the door open and dashed onto the porch.

Then he paused.

Lindsey glanced around, trying to figure out where the intruder had gone.

But it was almost like he was a ghost. There was

no one in sight. No noise. No clue as to which direction he'd disappeared.

Benjamin muttered under his breath and shook his head before running a hand through his hair.

"I'm sorry," he said as he turned to her. "He got away."

Lindsey wasn't sure what to say, but she was suddenly distracted by the cut on his forehead.

She reached up but didn't touch the wound. "You're hurt."

Benjamin reached for his cut also and then shrugged. "It's nothing."

"It doesn't look like nothing. Let's get you inside and get that cleaned up."

She was anxious to hear what had happened.

CHAPTER FOUR

AS BENJAMIN LEANED against the kitchen counter, he recounted to Lindsey everything that had occurred—which wasn't much except for the fact someone had pushed him down.

He should have been more on guard. He knew better.

All it had taken was one moment of distraction, and now he had a cut on his forehead and an ache in his ribs. But it could be much worse.

He could have a bullet in his skull.

He tensed at the thought of it. He'd spent years on the battlefield, and he knew how quickly life could change. All it took was one moment . . .

Lindsey dabbed his forehead with a white washcloth she'd brought with her. She'd wet it in the sink. "I'm so sorry this happened."

"It's not your fault." Her vanilla scent as she leaned toward him soothed his otherwise frayed nerves.

"What do you think that man was doing in the inn?"

"I wish I knew. I can go up there and see if he did any damage."

She frowned. "I doubt this place could be any more damaged. I just feel like this inn has always been a source of trouble."

Lindsey's words caught him off guard. Terrible things had happened here. But Lindsey's words held extra emotion.

As she examined his wound, Benjamin took the opportunity to examine her.

She really was beautiful. Her cheekbones were lovely and defined. Her greenish-blue eyes shone with intelligence and compassion. But they also held untold stories. Stories he wanted to hear.

Benjamin shoved his thoughts aside. Where had that come from? He'd come here to do a job. He couldn't get distracted, no matter how beautiful Lindsey might be.

He'd already had his heart broken once. The last

thing he wanted was to jump into another relationship—especially one with Lindsey.

For so many reasons. So, so many reasons.

AFTER LINDSEY HAD BANDAGED Benjamin's forehead, she let out a surprising yawn. The five-hour trip to get here must be catching up with her.

"We should probably go ahead and make sure everything is ready so you can get some shut-eye tonight," Benjamin said softly. "We're going to need all our energy if we're going to fix this place up in a reasonable amount of time."

"I agree." Lindsey stepped back. But part of her was disappointed that she and Benjamin couldn't continue their conversation. She had so many questions for him, so much she wanted to know.

All those things could wait for another time. It sounded like they were going to have plenty of opportunities to catch up over the next several weeks.

"Make sure you lock your bedroom door tonight," Benjamin said. "I'll check all the exterior doors here at the inn, but this wood is all so old that I'm not sure how much protection they're going to be. Hopefully, that guy who was here was just curious."

"That's the most likely scenario."

Benjamin nodded, but he didn't look totally convinced. Did he think there was more going on here?

Lindsey didn't know. She couldn't be sure. Her thoughts were too muddled after everything that had happened over the past couple of months.

But the one question that remained on her mind was: what if tonight's events had something to do with Colin? Was that even possible?

She thought the man had done his damage and was out of her life. But he'd been so angry with her. He'd spewed such hatred toward her. Said such awful things.

Now, what if he carried through with those threats?

Lindsey's heart thumped harder at the thought. She didn't even like to think about it. But she'd be a fool if she didn't acknowledge that possibility.

Benjamin walked her down the hallway and paused outside her room. At once, she was filled with visions from the past. Benjamin had been such a crucial part of her preteen years. Seeing him here now just brought it all back—the good and the bad.

She couldn't get over what a handsome man he had turned into. He'd always been mischievous, but now he actually gave off an air of being responsible and capable. The Benjamin she knew said he wanted to travel the world, but this grown-up Benjamin seemed so settled.

She hardly knew what to think.

Except that he had a lovely jawline and beautiful green eyes.

She cleared her throat, knowing with certainty that she needed to keep those thoughts to herself. "I still can't believe you're here."

"Yeah, I can't believe that I'm here either. It's like old times almost, isn't it?"

"It is. Except during old times, you'd tug my pigtails and tap me on the shoulder when I wasn't looking and do everything you could to annoy me."

He grinned and shrugged. "What can I say? My methods of flirting may not have improved."

Lindsey stared at him another moment before smiling. "I can't wait to hear all about your life."

He stared deeply into her eyes, something unspoken in the depths of his gaze.

She stepped back toward her room, realizing it would be better if she just went to bed. She couldn't trust any of her emotions right now. They were all too heightened.

"Good night, Benjamin." Her throat burned as she said the words.

"Good night, Lindsey."

He waited until she was inside her room. She then heard his footsteps as he walked toward the front of the inn, heading back, no doubt, to check the rest of the doors.

Knowing he'd turned out to be such a good person made it even harder to know how his teen years had been turned upside down . . . all because of Lindsey.

CHAPTER FIVE

BENJAMIN STARTED his day by grabbing a piece of toast and some coffee. When he'd awoken this morning, the electricity had been on.

That would make his job a lot easier.

He downed both the coffee and the toast before he even saw Lindsey.

He hoped she emerged soon.

If this place was going to be ready to either be utilized or put on the market anytime soon, he needed to get to work. As he'd been waiting for her to wake up, he'd removed some wood paneling from the wall and examined the electrical wires leading into the kitchen. None of them were up to code.

The entire place would need to be rewired. It wouldn't be a cheap fix either.

As Benjamin stared at the jumble of wires, he chewed on the thought a moment. They would have to get a licensed electrician out here to do the job. There was no way around it.

He let out a sigh as he stared at the wires. He hated to break the news to Lindsey.

But, certainly, she was smart enough to realize that this whole place was going to be a money pit. He wondered why Lindsey just didn't try to sell it as-is or why she hadn't done so in the years since her parents had passed away.

The inn didn't hold good memories for her, so he was surprised she'd held on to it for as long as she had.

Benjamin stepped back and closed his eyes for a minute, imagining what this place had looked like during the height of its grandeur. It had been quite the destination. Wealthy people from all over the East Coast had come here to enjoy the luxuries offered.

Then the place had eventually been sold to Lindsey's parents. The grandeur of the previous time period had ended, and the Eastern Shore was no longer as affluent as it had once been.

That's when the struggles with this place had

started. Ultimately, those struggles had led to the inn's demise.

Well, those struggles as well as everything that happened with Lindsey.

Benjamin heard a step behind him and turned. When he saw Lindsey there, he felt foolish. But, at once, his mind was transported back in time. To just last night. To the intruder he'd heard in the inn.

He'd hardly slept at all as he'd waited to hear more footsteps. As he'd waited to hear if the man had returned.

Because even though he'd played it off to Lindsey as if it hadn't been a big deal, whenever someone entered your private space without permission, it *was* a big deal.

Lindsey offered an almost shy smile as she muttered, "Good morning."

She stood there in some old jeans and a Shenandoah National Park T-shirt. Her hair had been pulled into a sloppy ponytail at the back of her head, and she'd slipped on some work boots—probably a good idea considering the state of this place.

However, she'd never looked so beautiful.

Benjamin chided himself again. This wasn't where his thoughts needed to go. He needed to keep them in check.

"Good morning," he started. "I have some bad news. Do you want me to wait until after you've had some coffee?"

She sighed before trudging across the floor to the coffeepot and grabbing a mug. She poured a cup and took a sip before turning to him. "I'm ready now."

He resisted a smile before launching into his issue with the electric wiring.

Lindsey pressed her lips together in thought when he finished. "You think that you can fix it?"

He let out a long breath. "It's a big task. An *expensive* task. If you want this place to be operational and meet building codes, you'll need to hire a licensed electrician to do the work."

She stared at the mess of wires in the wall and sighed. "I need to do this the right way. It's just that I don't have unlimited funds."

"Let me ask around and see if can find someone to help us. I need to go into town anyway to get a few supplies. I'll see what I can find out."

She pulled her gaze away from the wires and nodded. "That sounds fine. But I need to go over some things with you—including my budget."

"We might as well start with that now."

For the next hour, Lindsey reviewed her plans for the place. Thankfully, she wasn't knocking down any walls. The basic blueprint would stay the same. But she did want to refurbish the floors, repaint the walls, and update the bathrooms and kitchen.

Before they could do any cosmetic changes, they needed to make sure the electric and plumbing were in good shape, though.

When they finished, he stood. "Let me find an electrician first. Then you'll know how much money you have left in your budget."

"Sounds like a plan. I'll stay here and make a list of some things I can do in the meantime."

He paused before walking away and briefly remembered last night's intruder. "Are you sure that you're going to be okay here by yourself?"

She waved her hand in the air. "I'm sure. Don't worry about me."

Benjamin stared at her another moment, unsure whether or not to believe her bravado. Finally, he nodded. It was the middle of the day. Lindsey had a cell phone if she ran into any trouble.

Still, something about the idea of leaving her here alone didn't settle well with him. But there was no way the two of them could be around each other all the time. He had to get used to the idea that Lindsey was an independent woman and that he wasn't her guardian.

He finally stepped back and offered a nod. "I'll probably be back in an hour or so. If you need anything, please call."

He gave her his number, and she saved it on her phone before offering what looked like a forced smile.

With one more glance at her, Benjamin turned to leave, still feeling entirely more reluctant than he should.

LINDSEY WASN'T sure why she was doing everything that she was. Maybe it was simply because she couldn't figure out what to do or where to start. That's why she needed someone like Benjamin here.

Because this place was going to require more than just some redecorating.

It was going to need a total renovation. It wasn't just the wires that would need to be replaced. But probably the pipes, the HVAC, even some of the floorboards seemed soft. And then there were the windows and the roof.

She ran a hand through her hair. What was she thinking trying to fix this place up? It was going to take every cent of her savings to do so. She could just try to sell it as-is.

But she couldn't bring herself to do that. Some type of internal urging told her that to find closure on her past, she needed to do this. She couldn't explain it to anybody. And no one had really asked. Everyone back home had just assumed that she came here because of Colin. And he was the main reason.

But there was so much more to her story. So much more.

She let out a long breath and realized that she needed to step away from her cleaning for a moment in order to get her thoughts straight.

She grabbed one of the rugs from the living area, rolled it up and carried it out to the back deck. She would see if she could beat some of this dust out of it. The rug itself didn't appear to be in terrible shape. Maybe she could salvage it.

The summer sun hit her as she stepped onto the deck and draped the rug over the rickety railing there.

But it was the view that caught her eye.

It did every time.

As much as she had resented having to live here, the view of the Chesapeake Bay had always been a small beacon of hope for her.

Still to this day, the salty air surrounding her seemed to fill her lungs with warmth and ease her troubled thoughts.

If only it were that easy.

"Well, if it isn't Lindsey Waters," a scratchy voice said from a distance.

Lindsey startled at the sound. But even without looking, she knew who that voice belonged to.

"Irma Brickhouse," she muttered.

She turned to see a woman trudging across the grass, coming from the direction of the woods.

Irma's hands were clasped together in front of her, and a wide smile stretched across her face. Her graying hair was slicked back into a tight bun, and she wore a flowered dress that was probably thirty years old, but it still fit her petite frame.

She lived on the adjoining property in a small cottage, which had been the original carriage house when the inn was built more than a hundred years ago. Lindsey wasn't sure how Irma had gotten to the inn since a fence surrounded the place on three sides. Lindsey had a feeling some of the fencing had probably fallen down in recent years, giving anyone cutting through the woods easy access to the area.

"What are you doing back here?" Irma asked. "I heard the rumors, but I had to come myself to see if it was true."

"I'm going to fix this old place up."

"Well, isn't that wonderful." Her voice sounded almost sickly sweet.

Then again, it always had. Lindsey didn't even think the woman talked like that on purpose or to be fake. It was just how her voice sounded.

"Your mom and dad would be so happy if they were alive to see this," Irma continued.

At the mention of her mom and dad, Lindsey felt her stomach clench. She didn't like to talk about them, for various reasons.

That's when she decided to change the subject. "So, I assume you're still living next door?" Lindsey nodded in the direction of a small carriage house just up the shoreline.

Irma was the closest neighbor. The *only* neighbor, really.

"I am," Irma said. "I can't give this place up."

"And do you work at the library still?"

Irma shook her head. "Not anymore. I retired about five years ago."

"What do you do with your time now?"

"Easy. I read. I read a lot. And it's glorious."

An idea suddenly hit Lindsey, and she glanced at the inn. "Say, I know you like to keep an eye on things. Have you ever seen anything happening here at the inn?"

Irma stared at her a moment, blinking with curiosity. "You mean, like a ghost?"

"No, not a ghost." Lindsey had fallen for those stories as a child. But no more. "I mean, do any locals ever get bored and come out here? Or any kids head this way to start some trouble?"

Irma seemed to think about it a moment before shaking her head. "Honestly, it's pretty quiet around here. I don't see many people out here at all. And there's a gate at the entry, which makes it harder for people to get back here."

Lindsey frowned. "Right."

Irma continued to peer at her, her eyes glinting. "Any reason why you're asking?"

"Someone was inside the inn last night." Lindsey decided to dive in with the truth. "I was just wondering if I should be concerned."

"Is that right?" Irma clucked her tongue before shaking her head. "Probably just somebody snooping around this old place. It has so much history."

"Yes, it does. Yes, it does." But most of the history here shouldn't be remembered—only if it was being used as a lesson in how not to behave.

CHAPTER SIX

AS BENJAMIN GRABBED various items in the hardware store and placed them in his shopping basket, he felt someone's eyes on him. Since there was only one other person in this place, he knew it had to be the clerk standing behind the counter.

The man had nodded hello when Benjamin came inside. He was probably in his seventies. He wore coveralls and an old trucker hat. A well-used coffee mug sat in front of him, and he occasionally took a sip of the black liquid inside.

Benjamin knew all about small-town dynamics. And he knew that when strangers cruised into town they were often the subject of a lot of curiosity.

But the man behind the counter made no secret that he was watching Benjamin's every move.

Benjamin grabbed the last item on his list and carried his basket to the counter to check out. He offered his most affable smile to the clerk. "Good morning."

"Morning." The man spoke slowly, purposefully. The name on his coveralls read "Fred." "Hear you're staying at the Hidden Shores Inn."

"That's right. I guess word travels around town fast." Benjamin pulled out his wallet, though the man seemed in no hurry to check out his items.

"It does. We're real wary of strangers around here."

"Nothing wrong with that. It's only smart."

"Although . . . you're not really a stranger, are you?" Fred narrowed his eyes as he studied Benjamin.

"I guess not. I lived here a couple of years while in my early teens."

The man nodded slowly. Judgmentally? Maybe.

"I remember." Fred picked up the electrical tape from Benjamin's basket and began ringing him up. "Did I hear that Lindsey Waters is back too?"

Benjamin tensed. He wasn't sure how much Lindsey wanted people to know. He certainly didn't want to be the one to share anything meant to be private.

"She is." Benjamin hoped that affirmation was safe enough. Clearly, people in town were attuned to what was going on at Hidden Shores.

"Poor girl. I can't stop thinking about what happened to her." Fred clucked his tongue and rang a few more items through, each of his actions and words painstakingly slow.

"It was a real tragedy."

"Never did like the way her parents treated her." Fred shook his head. "They were tough on her. Real tough."

"They were." Benjamin didn't offer any more information. He didn't want to feed the rumor mill.

The man put Benjamin's last item into a paper sack. "Sorry about your father."

Benjamin rubbed his jaw. "Thanks."

To change the subject, Benjamin asked Fred for a recommendation on a local electrician. Fred offered the name of one guy—Howie Atticus—and also handed him a list of other contractors in the area in case they needed more help.

Fred hit a few keys on the register before turning back to Benjamin. "Well, good luck fixing that place up. As far as I'm concerned, that inn is nothing but bad news. In fact, if I were you, I'd run far away—far, far away."

Benjamin's throat tightened.

Maybe he had taken on more than he could handle. But it was too late to back out now.

AFTER LINDSEY REVIEWED some paperwork and her to-do list, she decided to walk around the inn and go room by room making notes.

She was going to start upstairs.

In the area where she'd heard that man walking last night.

Tension tightened around her spine with every step, especially when she remembered what had happened.

Someone had been up here, and she still had no idea why.

Her throat felt dry, but Lindsey told herself the reaction was ridiculous. She had no reason to be afraid. If someone else was in this old building, she would have heard them. This place creaked with every step and every time the wind blew.

As she continued up the stairs, her throat suddenly felt dry and sweat sprinkled across her forehead.

Maybe she should wait until Benjamin got back.

But there was no need. She was a grown woman. She could handle this.

With a touch of hesitation, Lindsey stepped toward the north wing and glanced at the dark corridor. Could this place be any creepier? Maybe—but only if it had old dolls to add to the eerie atmosphere.

As she stepped farther into the space, more memories of growing up here filled her mind. She tiptoed around now, just as she'd had to do when she was a child. Hospitality was very important to her parents, not to mention the fact that children should be seen and not heard. That had been emphasized many, many times.

Instead of starting at the first bedroom, she walked to the end of the hall, shuddering when she saw the portraits hanging on the walls. She didn't know most of the people portrayed, but their expressions seemed so somber and sad.

She hadn't liked the pictures as a child. She didn't like them now either. She'd always felt like those creepy eyes were watching her, moving along with her as she passed by.

She reached the last room of the hallway. It had always been her favorite. In between guests, Lindsey would stand on the balcony and stare out at the

Chesapeake Bay. That huge oak tree stood on one side still, almost seeming like a fortress within itself.

The door creaked open as she entered. All the furniture was covered with white sheets, giving the place a spooky feel. It was a good thing she didn't believe in ghosts.

She stepped inside farther and glanced around.

At once, she remembered all the fancy guests they used to have here. Guests that kept their noses up in the air as they dumped their luggage off on her.

Things like that weren't easy to forget.

She paced across the room, running her fingers along the dresser. Then she paused by an old closet door with a crystal handle. She used to always pretend those sparkling handles were diamonds and worth a lot of money.

Lindsey twisted the handle and opened the door. A stale, dusty scent rose around her. This space clearly hadn't been opened up in a while.

She stepped inside, turning on the flashlight on her phone. The wallpaper covering the walls was now peeling, revealing a sickly yellow backing.

Out of curiosity, she tugged at a corner to see how easily the paper would come off.

The whole section fell to the floor.

That settled that. This paper couldn't be preserved.

But as Lindsey glanced at the wall where the paper had once been, she saw words had been written there.

I didn't mean to do it. Please, forgive me. I beg you. Please!

A chill raced up her spine.

Who in the world had written that? And why?

CHAPTER SEVEN

AS SOON AS Benjamin returned from the hardware store, Lindsey showed him the words in the
closet.

*I didn't mean to do it. Please, forgive me. I beg you.
Please!*

"This is strange," he murmured as he hunched
down to examine the words more closely.

The scribbles *were* curious. The messages didn't
appear to be written by a child. The handwriting
was too neat. Too proper.

"Maybe it was a joke." Benjamin straightened
and stepped from the closet. "Maybe someone left
them there so people would ask questions later. A
friend of mine said he once buried a treasure map
beneath the deck of his house. He hoped one day

someone would find it and waste a whole bunch of time trying to find a treasure that didn't exist."

"Maybe." Lindsey nibbled on her bottom lip as she stood with her arms across her chest, leaning on the wall closest to the closet. "This whole place not only brings back bad memories, but it gives me the creeps."

Against his better judgment, Benjamin reached forward and squeezed her hand. "I know. I know."

His gaze caught hers, and Lindsey straightened, almost as if just realizing he'd touched her. Benjamin quickly pulled his hand away and shoved it into the pocket of his jeans.

"I was thinking . . . how about you and I work extra hard today," he started. "Then for dinner, I thought we could try the Seafood Shack. It's just down the street."

"I'm not really ready to face the people in this town . . ." She frowned almost apologetically.

"I thought you might say that. We can order something to pick up and bring it back here. Maybe we could sit on the deck tonight and eat and watch the sunset."

A smile flashed across her face. "That sounds wonderful."

Benjamin grinned. He'd been hoping for that

reaction. "Perfect. I'll get to work—I have a lead on an electrician—and then we can eat and have some time to unwind and catch up. I want to know what's been going on in your life since we last saw each other."

"I'd love to catch up with you also."

But as they walked away, questions lingered in Benjamin's mind. There was so much he didn't know. So much that didn't make sense.

He had a feeling there was entirely more to what was happening at the inn than he'd ever suspected when he took this job.

LINDSEY STAYED BUSY CLEANING, picking out paint colors, and looking at some tile samples she'd brought with her. She wasn't going to be much help as far as working on electrical wires or plumbing, but she'd always loved decorating.

She'd also put together a list of items she'd need to purchase—including paintbrushes, tarps, and some items to refinish the kitchen cabinets.

Her day had flown by surprisingly fast. She had to admit she was looking forward to dinner and having the chance to catch up more with Benjamin.

Her desire had nothing to do with those soulful eyes of his. At least, that's what she told herself.

Finally, at six o'clock, Lindsey called it a day. Benjamin offered to go pick up the food from the Seafood Shack. While he did that, she hopped in the shower and cleaned herself up enough to feel human.

When she stepped back into the kitchen area, she glanced around, noting that everything pretty much looked the same as it had when she arrived.

She and Benjamin hadn't even made a dent in their workload. Granted, they had a ton to do. But she just needed to know some progress was being made. Progress gave her hope to continue.

Be patient, Lindsey. Just be patient.

Just as she stepped outside onto the deck, Benjamin appeared from around the corner with a bag of food in hand. "I picked up some bottles of water as well."

"Perfect."

The two of them settled with their Styrofoam containers on an old picnic table. Lindsey had brought two towels outside with her and laid them across the seat so they wouldn't get splinters.

As they stared out at the bay, the sun sank closer to the horizon. The surrounding clouds seemed to promise the sunset tonight was going to knock it out of the park.

"I tried to find you, you know," Lindsey started before taking a bite of her crab cake sandwich.

Benjamin cast a quick glance at her. "You did?"

"I couldn't find you on social media. Somebody even told me that you changed your name after what happened to . . . your dad." Her throat burned.

She didn't want to bring up his dad. But how could she not? She didn't want the subject of what had happened to the man to remain the elephant in the room. Benjamin, however, hadn't seemed like he wanted to talk about it earlier, and she wanted to respect that.

"I like to stay off the grid." Benjamin picked up a fried clam and popped it in his mouth. This area was known for their littleneck clams.

"Did you ever go live on an island just like you always said you wanted to? Of course, you didn't want to live there for long. Just until you found your next adventure or a new way to make trouble."

He grinned. "As a matter of fact, I did. I moved to the Caribbean for a couple of years after my military service."

She picked up a french fry but, instead of eating

it, she just stared at him. "I never thought of you as the type who'd go into the military."

"I needed to do something with my life, and joining the Navy seemed like as good a choice as any."

As she noted the way his shoulders had filled out and his legs had stretched long and muscular, she figured that it had been good for him.

"I just can't believe you're back here," she murmured. "And I'm here. After all these years."

"Life has a funny way of coming full circle sometimes, doesn't it?"

"It sure does."

"What really brought you here?" He turned toward her, not hiding the curiosity in his gaze. "I hope you don't mind me asking. I just feel like there's more to your story."

Lindsey's jaw tightened at his question. She'd known it would come. The inquiry only made sense.

But she didn't want to answer. She wanted to pretend like the events of the past several months hadn't happened.

"That's a long story," she finally said. "Maybe I'll save that for another day."

Even though she and Benjamin had been close friends a long time ago, that didn't mean she needed to pour out her entire life story. It was best if no one here knew exactly what happened in Staunton.

"I understand." Benjamin took another bite of his dinner, and they stared off into the distance.

She let out a breath of relief.

She'd delayed the inevitable . . . for a little while longer, at least.

CHAPTER EIGHT

AFTER LINDSEY and Benjamin finished eating, they decided to take a walk along the edge of the cliff.

The inn was located on an eighty-foot-high bluff with an old wooden staircase that led down to the beach below. Even though erosion had taken away some of the land, a patch of grass spread between the inn and where the ground disappeared.

As they strolled, a million questions jostled in Benjamin's head. Just what was Lindsey hiding? He could see the secrets in her eyes. There were things she didn't want to talk about.

That was her right. She had no obligation to open up to him. But there was clearly more going on here than he knew.

They passed by the old tree, and he stared up at it.

This was the gigantic oak tree that had once earned this area its name, Hanging Hill.

A hundred fifty years ago, the town of Butler's Point had been located here. The area was apparently lawless, and town leaders had taken justice into their own hands.

When a man was caught holding a knife and his wife's dead body was lying in front of him, he'd been tried and convicted of murder on the spot. His sentencing? Death by hanging on this very tree.

Several other crimes had occurred throughout the years with similar results. People said if you looked up at one branch in particular, you could still see the grooves where the rope had once been wrapped.

When Lindsey's parents had bought this place, they'd quickly adopted the name Hidden Shores instead and had tried to put the town's morbid history behind them. But locals remembered.

It was something that shouldn't be forgotten lest history repeat itself.

Benjamin's gaze stopped at some letters carved on the trunk.

BN + LW

Lindsey seemed to see it at the same time he did and grinned.

"I remember when you carved that. So proud of yourself. The two of us . . . we were going to be best friends forever."

Best friends, huh? Nothing more? Benjamin didn't bring it up.

"Those were the days, weren't they?" he murmured, staring at the crude letters from simpler times.

"Yes, they were. You were my sanity." Lindsey stepped closer, openly observing him. "But something seems so different about you now. I keep trying to figure out exactly what it is."

His neck tightened with a sudden intensity, and he cleared his throat. "I guess we all change with time, don't we? Certainly, you're not the same either."

"No, but it's more than that. It's almost like you're a different person." Her intelligent eyes stared at him, almost as if she soaked in his every feature she might find an answer.

That was the last thing he wanted.

He swallowed his nerves. "I'm still me. Still Benjamin. I liked eating crayons when I was a kid. I still love tomato and cheese sandwiches. And back when we were kids, I thought you hung the moon."

She stared at him another moment before letting out a breath. Her lips curled up in a grin. "That sounds like the Benjamin I know. But there's still something that's different. One day, I'm going to pinpoint exactly what it is."

Benjamin hoped she couldn't see the heat rising up his cheeks.

Before he had a chance to say anything else, the sound of glass breaking filled the air.

Lindsey clutched his arm as she turned toward the noise. "What was that?"

"You stay here while I go find out."

LINDSEY WASN'T GOING to stay where she was. She needed to see with her own eyes what had just happened.

She followed him around the side of the inn and paused in the front yard.

One of the windows had been broken.

She glanced around and saw nothing suspicious. No one lingering in the shadows. No sticks that had fallen from the tree.

There was no explanation.

Except maybe a ghost.

But she still didn't believe in ghosts.

"Benjamin?" Her voice came out raspy.

He glanced back at her, his look clearly indicating she wasn't supposed to be here. Then he motioned for her to follow him onto the front porch. They opened the door and stepped inside.

As they turned toward the broken window, Lindsey spotted a brick on the floor near the shards of glass.

Someone had thrown a brick into her window?

The perpetrator must have run into the woods afterward. Lindsey hadn't heard the sound of any vehicles. Plus, the gate out front was locked.

At this point, whoever had done this was probably far away. He or she had most likely left a car on the side of the road, run through the woods, and jumped inside.

Benjamin knelt beside the brick. "It looks like there's a note around it."

Lindsey stepped closer for a better look. A paper was wrapped around the brick, held in place with a rubber band.

"Should we touch it?" she asked. "What if there are fingerprints?"

"I'll be careful." Benjamin took the edge of his shirt and pulled the rubber band off. Then, still using the edge of his shirt, he lifted the paper.

A message was scrawled there.

It read, "Get out while you can."

CHAPTER NINE

AS THEY WAITED for the sheriff to arrive, Benjamin fixed them each a cup of coffee. He was desperate to do something to make Lindsey feel better. The woman was obviously—and rightfully—shaken up right now.

They sat in the living room off the foyer, a grand space with a massive fireplace and huge windows overlooking the water. However, the furniture was stiff and dusty. With a little work, this place could be a real beauty again.

But Benjamin couldn't imagine the amount of money it would take to renovate everything. Lindsey didn't give him the impression that she had an abundance of money. In fact, her budget for this project was very modest.

He took a sip of his coffee and watched her. She stared off into the water, her mind clearly in another world.

"Someone really doesn't want me here." She picked up her coffee mug, but it trembled in her hands. She set it back down again and frowned.

"But why? That's what doesn't make sense to me. Why would someone want you out of town? How can you possibly be a threat to them?"

Her gaze latched onto his. "Maybe it has something to do with those two weeks I was missing."

His spine straightened as he waited to hear what else she had to say.

"I still don't remember anything about them." She stared out the window, her voice sounding wistful.

"You have no recollection at all about what happened during those days?"

She shook her head. "I don't. I thought for a while about going to a psychologist or someone who might be able to help me dig up those memories. But then I figured that maybe there was a reason I was supposed to forget."

"Or maybe you need to remember so you can move on." He said the words softly, not wanting to overstep. "So healing can truly begin."

She shrugged. "I don't know. There are no easy answers."

"That's true."

"But I do think about those missing weeks a lot. I haven't felt the same since then. The police said that there were no signs I was physically harmed. No cuts or bruises or signs of sexual assault. In fact, I was fed and hydrated while I was missing. So where was I? And why was I taken?" She stared at him as if he might have the answers.

"I wish I could tell you."

Lindsey's gaze looked even heavier than before. This whole conversation was clearly weighing her down.

Before they could talk more, Lindsey's cell phone rang, and she glanced at the screen. "It's the sheriff. I need to go let him in."

Benjamin stood. "Why don't you let me do that? You just wait here."

LINDSEY FELT like her insides were shriveling as she turned toward Sheriff Ross.

The man had been sheriff in this town for as long as she could remember. He'd been the one in charge of the investigation after she'd gone missing. He'd also been the one who charged Benjamin's father with her abduction.

"You look just as pretty as ever." Sheriff Ross stood in the grand foyer, his hand on his belt. The man was gangly, with a beak-like nose and beady eyes. His hair was thinning and grayish black, and each of his motions seemed calculated.

Lindsey stoically nodded. "Thank you."

He turned toward Benjamin and nodded, something flickering in his gaze. "Mr. Newsom."

Benjamin nodded back, his gaze hardening slightly.

Sheriff Ross looked at Lindsey again. "I heard you had an incident here at the inn."

Benjamin lifted up the brick that had been thrown inside. He'd put it in a plastic bag, careful in case there were any prints on it. "This was thrown through the window, which, as you can see, is broken."

Sheriff Ross glanced back at the shattered glass remaining around the window frame and frowned. "I saw that when I pulled up." He took the bag from Benjamin, held the brick to the light. "A brick?"

"There was a note around it too." Lindsey

showed him the paper she'd placed in another bag. "It said that I should leave now while I could."

The sheriff raised a shaggy eyebrow. "What does that mean?"

"I wish I knew. There was also someone in the inn last night, but he got away before we could catch him."

The sheriff's eyebrows shot up. "Definitely sounds like somebody doesn't want you here. Why would that be?"

Lindsey stared at him, something about the man grating on her nerves. Maybe it was his cocky demeanor or the way he spoke to her as if she was still a child. She couldn't be certain.

"To be honest, if I knew that I might not have called you to come out here," Lindsey finally said.

"I'll take these to the station and see if we can find any prints. But I wouldn't hold my breath."

"Don't worry, I'm not." Lindsey hadn't meant for her words to sound harsh, but they did.

The fact of the matter was that she didn't trust the sheriff to do a good job. It seemed like there was hardly any crime around here to begin with. The cases he had been handed, he seemed to fumble. That was her impression at least.

Just like the case centering around Benjamin's dad.

Lindsey shoved those thoughts aside for now.

Sheriff Ross continued to observe her, something calculated behind his gaze. "How long do you plan to stay here in town, Lindsey?"

She shrugged. "I figured I'd get this place fixed up. Then maybe I'll sell it. Maybe I'll keep it for a few years. I'm not sure yet."

His eyebrows shot up. "Is that right? Do you think somebody will buy a place like this? The Eastern Shore isn't what it used to be, you know."

Lindsey glanced around the space. "It's better than just letting the inn sit here and rot."

"To each their own." The sheriff shrugged. "Anyway, good luck to both of you. This is a big task. I'm not sure I'd want to tackle it. Most of the locals here in town don't want to work on this place. They still think it's haunted."

"I'm well aware." Lindsey felt more irritation straightening her spine.

With another nod toward her, Sheriff Ross raised the bags with the brick and the note again. "I'll make a report of this and get back with you. You might want to put some wood over that window."

"I plan on doing that," Benjamin said. "I just

thought you might want to document the incident first."

"I've documented that right up here." Sheriff Ross tapped his temple.

Lindsey resisted an eye roll. The only thing that made her feel better was knowing that Benjamin seemed to feel the same way about the man as she did.

They walked the sheriff out and then closed the gate before coming back into the inn.

"Let me grab some plywood, and I'll put it over this window," Benjamin said. "The good news is that you should replace these windows anyway with something more energy efficient."

"I'll take any good news I can get." But Lindsey heard the sarcasm in her voice. She didn't like it. But she was fighting hard right now to make the best of things.

Just like what happened back in Staunton, good intentions would most likely get her nowhere except for in a heap of trouble.

CHAPTER TEN

WHAT WAS GOING on in this town?

Why did it seem like everyone had a secret and ulterior motives? Even the sheriff. Benjamin didn't trust him as far as he could throw him.

Seeing the look of devastation on Lindsey's face . . . it was almost more than he could take.

Then when he'd heard her talking about the two weeks she'd been abducted . . . it had given him a new respect for her. She'd gone through a lot. Maybe too much.

Maybe Lindsey coming back to Hidden Shores wasn't a good idea. But Benjamin had a feeling that nothing he said to her could convince her of that.

He stood from the bed, unable to sleep. Instead, he paused at the window. Whoever had thrown that brick probably wasn't done yet. Would this person be back tonight?

Benjamin had no idea. He had no idea what the guy was planning at all.

He saw nothing outside other than the moonlight glinting on the water and the dark woods in the background. He dropped the curtain and paced back to his bed. He opened the nightstand drawer and pulled out a photo he'd placed there.

It was a picture of his cousin, Natalie. She was only eighteen.

Her dark hair had been pulled over her shoulders in a thick braid. Her eyes looked almost hollow and her skin entirely too pale.

But her smile still shone brightly, even in the midst of her fight.

Natalie needed his help. Desperately.

She had a heart condition, and Natalie's mom had found an experimental medical procedure that might help her. But it wasn't covered by insurance, which meant they had to foot the bill up front. And it was expensive. Really expensive.

Taking this job was one of the only ways Benjamin knew to get Natalie the help she deserved.

He only wished he could tell Lindsey all that. But he couldn't. Too much was on the line.

He put the photo back into the drawer and closed it. He didn't want Lindsey to ask too many questions.

But he still couldn't sleep.

It was too late to keep working on any projects. But he needed something to occupy his thoughts.

Just as he stepped out into the hallway, ready to quietly walk down toward the living area, he saw a shadow in the distance.

His breath caught.

Someone else was in the inn.

This time, Benjamin was going to catch him.

LINDSEY HEARD a creak behind her in the hallway and braced herself.

What was that sound?

Quickly, she darted behind a corner out of sight. Though she'd like to believe she was the type who could confront an intruder head-on and demand to know what he was doing in her place, she wasn't.

She was too slight and not nearly athletic enough to take down somebody. All the wishing in the world wouldn't change that.

Instead, she pressed herself into the wall and waited. As she did, her heart pounded in her chest.

She wished she'd brought her phone with her. Or maybe even that big brass candlestick she'd found last night.

But she had neither of those things. Lindsey had simply thought she'd go into the living room, find an old book on the shelf, and read for a while. She had too much on her mind to stay in bed.

But coming out of her room had been a bad idea.

She barely heard the footsteps as they came toward her. How had someone even gotten into this building again? She'd checked all the doors and windows herself before she'd gone to bed.

She pressed her eyes shut. *Lord, help me. I don't know what I'm doing.*

The footsteps stopped.

Lindsey braced herself, wondering what the person was doing.

The next instant, a man appeared around the corner. He held a lamp over his shoulder ready to swing at her.

She swallowed back a scream and ducked, ready to fight for her life.

Until she recognized him.

"Benjamin?"

His eyes widened, and he lowered the lamp. "Lindsey?"

She straightened, scolding herself for cowering. "It's me."

He set the lamp on the floor and shook his head before letting out an airy, almost self-deprecating chuckle. "I can't believe it's you."

"And I can't believe it's you," she echoed. She shivered as she remembered the fear that had captured her. The same fear she'd experienced that night years ago when a hand had covered her mouth. When everything had gone black. When her memories had disappeared.

"I'm sorry." Benjamin frowned. "I saw a shadow and thought it was an intruder."

His explanation made sense. Lindsey would have done the same thing. "I couldn't sleep so I decided to come out here to unwind. It seems like we're both on edge."

"It seems like we are." His understanding expression was also filled with regret—regret that they both had been forced to live with such apprehension.

"Do you want to sit out here and talk?" She nodded to a couch near the fireplace.

"Sure, I'd love to."

They sat on the old couch—which was in no way comfortable with its stiff cushions and wooden frame. Lindsey flipped on a lamp and light spilled from it, offering a small bit of illumination.

She was actually happy to have some company. Being alone with her thoughts was almost too much for her to handle.

"I have a question for you." Benjamin leaned forward, the gentle light softening his features.

"Shoot."

"Do you remember that trunk? The one we saw when we snuck outside to see the bioluminescence?" His words almost sounded tentative, as if he were walking on eggshells.

Caution filled her. "You mean the trunk we saw right before I was abducted?"

"That's the one. Whatever happened to it? Do you ever wonder why it was on the back deck?"

"I've thought about it a few times. It was weird." As Lindsey said the words, she touched the skeleton keys at her throat. "But I've never forgotten about it. That's why I collect these."

He leaned closer as if trying to get a better look in the dim lighting. "You collect skeleton keys because of that trunk?"

She shrugged. "Honestly, sometimes I feel that if

I'd opened that trunk, I would have all the answers I need today."

"Maybe that's your subconscious way of saying you need to unlock some old memories."

She grasped the keys harder. "Maybe, *Dr. Newsom.*"

A quick smile fluttered over his lips before disappearing just as quickly. "Had you ever seen it before that night?"

"No, never. You?"

Benjamin shook his head. "No, I hadn't seen it either. But I've been curious about it ever since. I've always wondered if it had anything to do with your abduction."

Lindsey's gaze cut to his. "You were there that night. You didn't see anything?"

A shadow fell over his gaze. "No, I didn't. I'm sorry."

Lindsey crossed her arms. "We never really talked after that, you know? I was missing, and then I showed up again here at the inn. But, by that point, you'd been sent to live with other relatives. I always regretted the fact we weren't able to have any closure."

"I knew you were my friend." Benjamin's voice was unwavering with truth and reassurance. "That was always real."

"I know it was."

She opened her mouth, wanting to say more. But before she could, the room went pitch black.

"Benjamin?" Her voice came out in a shaky whisper.

"It's okay. I'm right here."

"Something's wrong. It's not storming outside." She supposed it could be the faulty wiring or maybe even a rat.

Or someone could have done this.

"I'll go check it out." Benjamin rose.

Lindsey rushed to her feet and glanced at the darkness around her. "I'll go with you. No way you're leaving me alone here."

CHAPTER ELEVEN

BENJAMIN STEPPED OUTSIDE, Lindsey on his heels.

He didn't mind. It was better if she stayed close, especially since he didn't know what was going on.

That familiar voice continued in his head. *You should have never taken this job.*

He silenced the nagging words as he continued outside, gripping his phone in his hands. He pulled up the flashlight on the device so he could see better. The darkness on this lonely stretch of water felt overwhelming at times.

Deck boards creaked beneath his feet as he stepped from the back door and walked toward the steps leading to the grass below.

Everything was quiet outside. Even the wind remained silent at the moment.

There was no good reason for the electricity to go out. Then again, the place needed to be rewired, and in these old buildings it was nearly impossible to predict what was behind the walls until those walls were torn open.

"Benjamin?" Lindsey's quiet voice cut through the silence. She clung to his arm, her vanilla scent offering a quick moment of comfort.

"I need to check out the electrical panel."

"Okay." She said the word quickly and quietly.

Benjamin heard the fear in her voice. Anyone in their right mind would be shaken up about everything going on here. He couldn't fault her for that.

Finally, they reached the box. As soon as he saw it, Benjamin knew what happened.

The cover had been torn off, exposing the wires beneath—wires that had been cut.

He shook his head as he muttered, "Someone did this on purpose."

Lindsey gasped. "What? Why?"

"Somebody didn't want us to have any power."

She glanced through the darkness surrounding them. "Whoever is trying to send a message is being pretty aggressive."

"I'd say." Benjamin swung his light around. The person who'd done this couldn't be that far away. It had been less than five minutes since the power went out.

Was this the same person who'd thrown a brick and run earlier? It only made sense.

Fingers dug into his arm. Lindsey was clutching his bicep, he realized. Her breathing was just a little too shallow for his comfort. He probably needed to get her inside.

Before he could, a noise in the distance caught his ear.

It almost sounded like a stick cracking.

In the woods.

"Did you hear that?" Lindsey whispered, her voice sounding thin with fear.

"I did."

Then he heard it again. The sound had *definitely* come from the woods.

Benjamin turned toward her. "I have to see who is behind this. Stay here. Please."

"But . . ." Lindsey couldn't even finish the statement. She probably realized that this was the best way.

What she didn't realize was that Benjamin's years of military experience had taught him the necessary survival skills he needed. He was no longer the teenager with a bent toward the mischievous. He . . . well, he wasn't the person she thought he was—on more than one level.

"Stay here," he muttered.

Then he took off toward the sound, determined to find some answers.

LINDSEY PRESSED herself into the side of the inn, an overwhelming sense of fear filling her. She could hardly breathe. Her skin felt clammy. Her pulse pounded so hard she felt certain anyone nearby could hear it.

Who had done this? Why couldn't he or she just let things go? Lindsey supposed this person was simply making it clear Lindsey wasn't welcome back here at Hidden Shores.

What exactly had gone on behind the scenes when she'd been a child? There were clearly things that her mom and dad hadn't told her. They'd been so distant. Always. But especially during the six months or so before her abduction.

Had money been tight? Had they been talking about getting a divorce?

She didn't know, and it was too late now to find out what any of those worries were. Her parents were both dead.

Her senior year of college, they'd been killed in a car accident while driving on an icy mountain road. She'd officially become an orphan in the blink of an eye.

But her mom and dad had left her this place—a place no one else ever wanted to touch. In fact, the building had been for sale for a while, but there'd never been any offers.

Her parents had changed after they'd left Hidden Shores. They seemed to have left behind part of themselves.

Lindsey stared in the direction Benjamin had run. The sound of his footsteps had faded away, and she hadn't heard anything else.

Woods lined her property, opposite of where Irma lived. If Lindsey remembered correctly, there was at least a mile of undeveloped shoreline to the north.

Lindsey supposed some people loved that. For others, it would be unnerving.

"Come on, Benjamin. Where are you? Are you okay?" She remained outside, her back against the wall as she waited.

She closed her eyes and lifted up a prayer.

Then another thought hit her. What if this wasn't about somebody here in town wanting her to leave? What if someone from Staunton had followed her here? What if they were determined to drive her away wherever she went? Maybe they wanted to make her pay for the mistakes she'd made back at her previous home.

A small cry escaped. Part of her couldn't even blame them.

She wiped beneath her eyes, trying to control her emotions.

Just as she did, she heard rustling in the woods again.

Somebody was coming back. Coming toward her.

Was it Benjamin?

Or was it the person he'd chased?

CHAPTER TWELVE

BENJAMIN EMERGED FROM THE WOODS, tension threading through his muscles. His leg ached from where he'd scraped it while running past a tree. Mostly, he was upset because he hadn't been able to catch that guy.

Lindsey met him before he even reached the inn. Worry filled her gaze. "Are you okay?"

He paused in front of her, shifting his weight to his uninjured leg. "He had a motorcycle waiting on the other side of the woods. He was halfway down the road before I got out of the woods."

"Could you tell anything about him? Or did you see a license plate number? Anything that might help us identify him?"

Benjamin shook his head, his jaw set. "I wish

there had been something. But, no, I couldn't make out any details. I'm sorry, Lindsey."

She nibbled on the side of her lip, almost as if holding back a frown. "It's okay. Thank you for trying, and I'm glad that he didn't hurt you."

His leg ached again, but he didn't mention that to her. She was too concerned as it was. There was no need to add more worries to her.

"I think we should get back inside." He nodded toward the inn.

"Of course. We don't have any electricity, but we can be thankful it's not too hot outside tonight—not that I plan on opening any windows."

He couldn't blame her for that. He wasn't sure he'd be opening his window either. Not out of fear. But he didn't want anyone surprising him while he slept either.

Benjamin walked Lindsey to her bedroom door, still using his phone as a flashlight and shining the beam in front of him. As they paused there, he turned and searched her gaze.

The rush of attraction he felt for Lindsey surprised him. He'd known she was beautiful and kind. But he hadn't come here looking for romance. He'd come here to do a job.

He quickly swallowed before he let the impulse

get the best of him. Instead, he shoved one hand into his pocket and stepped back.

"I have a good lead for an electrician," he said. "Fred at the hardware store gave me a name. We'll get those details worked out tomorrow. In the meantime, if you need anything, you know where I am."

Lindsey pushed a strand of hair behind her ear as she nodded. "Will do. Thank you. For everything."

Unrest clashed inside his chest.

Benjamin wondered if she would be thanking him once she learned the whole truth.

HOWIE ATTICUS, the electrician, showed up first thing in the morning. Lindsey wasn't sure if she'd ever been so happy to see someone, especially considering the fact she hadn't been able to make any coffee without electricity.

Howie appeared to be in his mid-forties. He had a dark beard and a mustache that curled on the ends. He wore well-worn jeans and an unbuttoned flannel with a T-shirt beneath it that read "Rebel." A toolbelt was strapped to his waist, and he had a friendly smile that put her at ease.

"Sorry to hear about the electrical problems

you're having here," he started. "I'll see what I can do to get you back up and running again. I'm assuming that's your first priority?"

Lindsey nodded and glanced at the two-story ceiling above her. The large crystal chandelier hung there like a ghost of sorts. "Yes, it is. But I understand that most of the wiring in the inn will have to be redone."

"That's my professional opinion," Benjamin added.

"I'll take a look at it. I can give you an estimate on how much it will cost to get it all fixed. But based on the size of the building," Howie glanced around, "it's not going to be cheap."

Lindsey frowned. She'd anticipated this would be expensive—and Benjamin had warned her. But she really didn't want to use most of her budget on this.

She might not have any choice, however.

"I'm not anticipating it will be cheap," she finally said. "But with no electricity, this place is no good to anyone. Plus, I know it won't pass inspection."

"I'll get you an estimate written up—just as soon as I restore the power." Howie paused again and glanced around one more time. "Yeah, I remember hearing stories about this place when I was growing up."

Lindsey paused and studied him for a moment. He didn't seem familiar to her. "You grew up around here?"

"Not too far from here. About thirty minutes north. I used to hear my parents talk about the inn when I was a kid. I heard it had become rundown in recent years, but I had no idea it was this bad."

Benjamin glanced around before frowning. "To say the least."

"It's a shame. I can tell people used to have good times here. They don't put in chandeliers like that unless they want people to come and appreciate them." Howie let out a long breath. "All right, let me get out there and see what's going on."

"I actually think that I'm going to run into town and try to find a decent cup of coffee," Lindsey said. "Can I get something for either of you?"

"I'll take some coffee," Benjamin said. "A large, please."

"And an eclair too?"

Lindsey stared at him, but nothing registered on his face. Had she remembered incorrectly? He used to go crazy for eclairs. They were his favorite treat ever.

Eclairs had been at the top of his food chart, while nuts of any sort were at the bottom—he was allergic.

"Sure, I'll take an eclair," he finally said. But his words somehow sounded unconvincing.

Strange. It almost seemed like he didn't remember the detailed conversations they'd had about eclairs. Had so much happened in the years between them that he'd forgotten?

It was a good possibility. After his dad had been arrested, Benjamin had gone off to live with his aunt. His dad had died of a heart attack after only a week in jail.

People still claimed Mr. Newsom was guilty in Lindsey's abduction.

Lindsey thought he was an easy scapegoat, especially since he was no longer around to defend himself. But to the day he died, he'd proclaimed his innocence.

There was really still so much Lindsey didn't know about Benjamin. About his life after his dad's incarceration and death.

Either way, it didn't matter.

All that mattered right now was getting some coffee.

CHAPTER THIRTEEN

BENJAMIN'S HEART was still thumping in his chest twenty minutes after Lindsey left.

He tried to pay attention to what Howie was telling him about the knob and tube wiring, but all he could think about was how he'd clearly missed something.

The way Lindsey had brought up the eclair made it certain there was some type of history or story behind it.

But he didn't know what, and it was too late to find out.

Benjamin's throat tightened at the realization.

He should just tell her everything. He knew he should.

Lindsey wasn't anything like he'd thought she'd

be. Maybe he assumed she'd be broken. Or cold toward him after the accusations against his family. Or calloused after the bad hand she'd been given.

But she was none of those things. Instead, she was quick to smile. She was kind, compassionate. And she'd made something of her life.

Now Benjamin felt like he'd been put in an impossible position.

As soon as Benjamin had the chance, he was going to call Dawson Smith back. He would tell the man he wanted out of their agreement.

It would be best for all of them. Benjamin could leave this neglected old inn. Find another way to make the money he needed. Maybe Lindsey would realize this whole place was a gigantic fire trap. Maybe she'd move on, away from this town where she wasn't wanted.

Someone had made that clear.

Benjamin didn't believe in giving in to the demands of bullies. But, in this case, Lindsey's safety seemed to be on the line.

This place wasn't worth her life.

"So, what do you say?"

Benjamin looked up and remembered Howie had been talking as he'd examined the electrical panel outside. Unfortunately, Benjamin hadn't heard a word the man said. "Can you repeat that?"

Howie nodded at the panel. "Just a few more fixes, and you should be up and running again."

"I'm sure Lindsey will be happy to hear that."

Howie studied him for a moment, his gaze unapologetic as he used needle-nosed pliers to twist some wires. "You know, I'm surprised you came back to this area."

Benjamin felt himself bristle. "What exactly are you implying?"

Howie raised his hand as if to urge Benjamin to slow his thoughts, that he'd meant no offense. "I just think it's weird that both you and Lindsey are back here now again after all these years. That's all."

"Sometimes revisiting the past isn't a bad idea." Even as he said the words, Benjamin didn't know if he believed them.

Because, whether or not his background was connected to this inn, his past contained painful memories—memories he wanted to put behind him.

But he wasn't sure if that would be for the best.

LINDSEY TRAVELED INTO TOWN, past an old strip mall she vaguely remembered going to as a child. Back then, there had been a laundromat there as well as a convenience store, computer shop, and Chinese restaurant.

Today, one of those storefronts was now a coffeeshop.

She pulled into the lot, put her car into Park, and headed toward the door. The outside had been painted a teal color and light-up signs with coffee cups graced the windows.

As soon as she walked inside, the scent of coffee and vanilla filled her senses, instantly putting her at ease.

A woman probably only a few years younger than Lindsey stood behind the counter. She had blonde hair that had been pulled back into a baseball cap and wore a black apron stained with powdered sugar and cinnamon. She held a can of whipped cream in her hands as she smiled up at Lindsey.

"How can I help you?" the woman called.

Lindsey placed her order and then waited, browsing the local artwork scattered on the walls.

"I don't think I've seen you around here before,"

the barista said, glancing up from the coffee machine. "You just passing through?"

"I'm actually fixing up the inn up the road."

The woman's eyes widened. "That old place? I heard that somebody was trying to renovate it. Your parents used to own it or something, right?"

Lindsey nodded, briefly wondering what else the woman had heard. "That's right. It sounds like it's been the talk of the town?"

The barista shrugged. "I guess you could say that. Then again, sometimes folks around here don't have much else to talk about except other people."

"Oh, I understand. How long have you lived here?" Lindsey abandoned looking at the artwork and paced toward the counter instead.

"Born here. Moved away when I was nine. Came back three years ago."

"I'm Lindsey Waters." She narrowed her eyes as she tried to put together a mental timeline. "I'm surprised I don't recognize you. I'm guessing you're probably a few years younger than me, but in a town this small, it seems like we would have gone to school together or something."

"I'm Maple. My mom was Annie Myers. Anyway, she and I moved away about sixteen years ago. I was homeschooled, so our paths wouldn't have crossed there."

"I see."

Maple set Lindsey's order on the counter with a friendly smile. "Welcome back, Lindsey. I hope to see you around again."

Lindsey hoped that she might run into Maple again also. The woman actually seemed like someone Lindsey wouldn't mind getting to know a little better.

She carefully climbed back into her car with the coffee. As soon as she was inside with the door closed, her phone beeped. She wondered if it was Benjamin, texting to update his order. *Too late, buddy.*

But when she glanced down, she saw a text from an unknown number.

The words caused her blood to go cold.

I KNOW **who you are and what you've done. How can you live with yourself knowing their blood is on your hands?**

LINDSEY'S HEART BEAT HARDER. Who had sent this?

She glanced around, almost feeling as if somebody were watching her now.

With a quick glance at the window of the coffeehouse, she saw Maple standing close, dusting off a shelf. The woman waved to her before continuing to work.

Was it Maple she'd felt watching her?

Or was there entirely more going on here than met the eye?

CHAPTER FOURTEEN

BENJAMIN NOTICED Lindsey seemed a little shaken when she returned with coffee and an eclair, but he decided to ask her about it later. Howie was waiting for him to come and help.

Instead, he scarfed his eclair down and got back to work.

The electrician was certainly a talkative guy, an open-book type who seemed to share everything without embarrassment or remorse.

"That was crazy about Lindsey's disappearance fifteen years ago, wasn't it?" Howie lowered his voice as he leaned on the ladder and threaded an electrical wire through a small opening they'd made in the wall.

Benjamin's curiosity rose as he stood near

another opening farther down the wall. "I'd say. Not being able to remember two weeks of your life . . . I can't even imagine."

"Me either. The whole town went mad afterward." Howie sent him a wide-eyed look to drive home his words.

"Did it?" Curiosity spiked in Benjamin.

Howie stole another glance at him. "I suppose you were probably too young to remember."

"I was fourteen."

"So maybe you remember some of it. But you left not long afterwards, if I recall correctly."

"That's right. I wasn't around, and I only heard what my aunt told me, which wasn't much." Benjamin continued to pull the wire through as Howie pushed it.

"Things like children being abducted aren't supposed to happen in small towns like this. It was crazy."

Child abductions were a tragedy wherever they happened, Benjamin mused. "What do you think of this town anyway? I'm trying to figure it out. You know, now that I'm an adult, I can see it differently. There's a lot that doesn't make sense to me."

"I can tell you this. This place has secrets. And so does everybody who lives here."

The ominous sound of his words didn't do anything to comfort Benjamin. Exactly what did this guy mean by that?

"What kind of secrets?" Benjamin braced himself for the man's answer.

Howie motioned for Benjamin to move down to the next section of wall so they could continue. "Once you're around for a while, you'll figure the people here out. It's just everyone knows every-thing in towns like this. If you're new . . . you'll never be an insider. You'll never be able to join the club."

"There's a club?"

"There's not an official club. But you know what I mean. The good old boys club. The people who make all the decisions in town." Howie rolled his eyes as he explained.

Benjamin tried to sound casual as he asked, "Who's in charge of this club?"

"If I had to guess, I'd say the sheriff heads it up."

"Sheriff Ross?" The man's image filled his mind, and Benjamin found himself reacting with a scowl.

"The one and only. The man is interesting, to say the least."

Benjamin's curiosity spiked. He wasn't normally the type who liked to gossip. But he *would* like to find out more information so he could see exactly what he'd gotten himself into.

"Are you saying that the sheriff isn't someone you admire?" He continued to pull the wire through the wall.

"I just remember way back when, I was probably a teenager myself, he had an affair with a woman in town. When the news came out about it, it was a big deal. Yet, somehow, he still remained sheriff. Seems like that moral failure would be cause for him not to keep the job. But it seemed it was all about who you know—then and now."

A better image of the sheriff began to form in his mind. "Interesting. Why didn't you leave if you don't like it here that much?"

"The people in this town have always used scare tactics to get their way, some dating back to the very tree outside the inn where public hangings would take place." Howie locked his gaze with Benjamin's. "No one is going to scare me away. No one."

LINDSEY HAD JUST FINISHED PAINTING one of the walls when she heard a car pull up outside. Since Howie was still here, she'd left the gate open so anyone could come and go. But she fully intended on closing it as soon as she could.

She glanced out the window and saw the sheriff had arrived.

She wiped her forehead, knowing there was probably grime and paint streaking her skin. But there was nothing she could do about that now.

Lindsey reached the door right as a knock sounded. As she opened it, she plastered on a pleasant smile. She was going to play nice, but she'd never turn a blind eye again to an injustice. No amount of posturing would do the trick.

"Sheriff. I wasn't expecting you to come by again."

"Good afternoon, Ms. Waters." He looked her up and down before frowning. "Looks like you've been . . . busy."

It was a good thing she wasn't trying to impress anyone. "To say the least. Would you like to come in?"

"No need to do that. I just came by to give you a little update."

She crossed her arms, bracing herself for whatever he had to say. "What's going on, Sheriff?"

He let out a breath before launching into the announcement. "Unfortunately, we haven't been able to track down the person who threw that brick. But we *did* get a hit on a fingerprint."

Her lungs froze as she waited for him to continue. "Is that right?"

"It's someone named Leo Berlinski."

Her breath caught at the familiar name. "Leo?"

The sheriff's snake-like gaze narrowed in on her. "I take it you know him."

"I know his father." Memories tried to pummel her, but Lindsey kept them at arm's length, not wanting to give the sheriff any more information than she had to. She wasn't ready to share that story with anyone.

"Have you seen Leo or his father recently?"

She shook her head. "Not in a couple of months."

"Any reason why this man might want to throw a brick at you?"

"Honestly, I only met Leo a couple of times. But I worked with his father at my job in the Staunton area."

"Did his father have any reason to not like you?"

Heat rose inside her. "He wasn't my biggest fan. He owned the company, and I worked as a marketing specialist for him. Things went south, and his company ended up being shut down."

"I see." Finally, the sheriff nodded slowly, his expression pensive and guarded. "I'll keep my eyes open for him. I'm not sure why someone like Leo would throw a brick and tell you to leave this area, especially if he doesn't live here."

Lindsey shivered and nodded. It didn't make much sense to her either. She was really going to need to think this through.

"We'll keep working on it." Sheriff Ross tilted his head toward her. "In the meantime, you have a great time fixing up this old place. Every time I look at this inn, I always think if these walls could talk, we'd have some tales that would make a blockbuster movie . . ."

Lindsey rubbed her throat.

The sheriff was right. If these walls could talk, she was sure they'd have stories to tell.

However, the stories just might send chills down a person's spine.

CHAPTER FIFTEEN

THE NEXT TWO days passed uneventfully.

Benjamin couldn't believe how peaceful they'd been.

When he'd first arrived, the string of mishaps that occurred made him halfway expect the pattern to continue. Part of him felt relieved, like maybe those were all empty threats meant to scare Lindsey off and, when they didn't work, the person behind them had given up. The other part of him thought that was too good to be true, and he was just waiting for the other shoe to drop.

He and Howie had worked together on the electric wiring. When Benjamin had extra moments, he'd explored the inn, maybe more than he should have. But he was curious about the history of this place. Curious about Lindsey's story. Curious about whether or not that trunk was still in this inn.

At the moment, he flipped some burgers on the grill. He and Lindsey had started a comfortable routine of eating dinner together in the evenings. Since it was nice outside—as it had been for the past few nights—they ate on the deck and watched the sunset over the bay together. It had quickly become his favorite part of the day.

A rush of guilt filled him when he realized he didn't deserve to find any enjoyment in this job. Not with the secrets he hid.

Thankfully, he and Lindsey hadn't had too many deep conversations. It was best if they didn't. At least, in some ways it was best. Deep conversations offered too many opportunities for him to slip up, to say the wrong thing.

He finished cooking the last burger, turned the gas grill off, and then carried the plate to the table.

Lindsey had just finished setting out some chips, water, and fruit. Today, they were eating a late lunch/early dinner. Howie had been called to another job and wouldn't come back until closer to four, so Lindsey and Benjamin decided to take a break earlier.

She looked up at him as he placed the plate in front of her. "Those burgers smell delicious."

"My stomach is grumbling for one now."

"Then let's eat." She lowered herself into one of the old wooden chairs there.

He lifted a prayer for their food and then they dug into their dinner. They sat at the table and watched as cumulus clouds graced the bright blue sky and the bay glimmered and twinkled as if it had a secret it was dying to share.

"You know, I've been thinking about the conversation we had a few days ago, and I think you're right." Lindsey set her hamburger back onto her plate as she turned toward him. Her appetite seemed to have waned under her heavy thoughts.

Benjamin had no idea what Lindsey was talking about. "Right about what?"

"I thought I wanted to keep all my memories locked away. But maybe that's not the best thing for me to do at all." Lindsey touched her necklace, tugging at the keys there.

His breath caught. "What brought this about?"

"I guess I've had a lot of time to think since I came here. Part of the reason I came back to Hidden Shores was because I wanted closure."

He waited for her to continue.

A few minutes later, she did. "I could have just sold this place. I could have taken my savings and started somewhere fresh. But part of me wants to remember what happened to me during those two weeks I was gone. I want to unlock whatever memories there are."

"How do you plan on doing that?"

"I'm not sure." She glanced behind her at the inn. "I can't help but wonder if this place has some answers for me."

His spine tightened. "Do you think there are answers inside the inn?"

"I don't know. But I feel like the answers as to what happened to me can be found here. Either in this inn or in this town."

"That makes sense. You were found here in this town, weren't you?"

She nodded and put down her burger. "I was found by a hunter in the woods just outside of town. I could have easily died there."

"What's the first thing you remember?" Benjamin shifted to better see her.

"I remember being snatched. The next memory I have is of when I was rescued. Whatever happened in the time in between seems to have been erased from my memories."

"Is it amnesia?"

She shrugged. "Maybe it's partly amnesia, but I vaguely remember the doctor saying something about me being drugged. That's probably the main reason why things are so hazy for me."

"Do you ever have a glimpse of memories?"

Her fingers continued to play with the keys at her neck. "Not really. Every once in a while, I feel like something is trying to claw its way to the surface. But then the memory disappears. The whole experience makes me anxious, so I never try to fully dive into the process."

Benjamin pressed his lips together, wondering if he'd do the same thing in her shoes. "That's understandable. I hope you find some of those answers."

"Me too." She frowned.

Benjamin knew he couldn't push her any harder. Not now.

Because seeing the sadness in her gaze made him want to fight with everything in him to make her smile again.

LINDSEY NIBBLED on some fruit as she sat on the deck, letting a gentle wind release the tension in her muscles.

It had felt surprisingly good to open up to Benjamin. It had been a long time since Lindsey had let herself be open with anyone.

Her parents had never encouraged her to talk about what happened. They'd pushed her to move on. Lindsey had a couple of good friends she'd shared her story with. But mostly, she'd kept what happened private.

Then she'd trusted Colin. In the end, she shouldn't have. He'd only used his relationship with Lindsey as a way of distracting her from what was really going on at his company. She shouldn't have ever allowed herself to fall for his charms.

As a result of that, people had died.

That wasn't something Lindsey would ever forgive herself for.

"What did you do before you came here?" Benjamin shifted on the wooden bench and draped his arm across the back of it.

Any other time, Lindsey might have marveled at how handsome he looked with the sun flooding his skin and illuminating his subtle blond highlights. Or with his muscles rippling

THE INN ON HANGING HILL   125

beneath his shirt. Or his hair falling into his eyes.

But his question had caused her appetite to completely disappear.

Despite that, to buy time, she nibbled on another piece of fruit. Lindsey wasn't a fan of secrets. Clearly, people around here had secrets—secrets that hurt people. That wasn't what she wanted for her own life. Yet opening up about Colin could make her feel so off-balance.

Still, sometimes, secrets felt like burdens and unloading them could do a world of good.

She dragged in a breath, unsure exactly how deep she was going to go with her story. But she'd at least give Benjamin the CliffsNotes version.

"A year and a half ago, I started working for a wood mill out in Staunton, Virginia. I was hired to do marketing for the company. It was a good-sized operation, and the company was using some cutting-edge technology. They did more than just mill the lumber. They'd developed this treatment process that preserved the wood."

"Okay . . ." Benjamin leaned toward her, his rapt attention on her every word.

"As part of my job, I went into town to talk to people there and get their thoughts on the business.

I thought they'd all say glowing things about the company and how it had brought jobs to the area. Instead, I got more than I bargained for." A sickly feeling gurgled in her stomach.

"What did they say?"

Lindsey let out a long, pent-up breath. "They started telling me about all the people in town who'd gotten sick since the mill opened up. They all thought their illnesses were tied with the mill, but they said no one believed them."

"What did you think?" Benjamin's voice held an edge of curiosity.

She shrugged. "I didn't know what to think. Honestly, it sounded outlandish. I'd met the people who worked at the company, and they all seemed above reproach. So, I brushed these people's statements off. It was around that same time that Colin asked me out."

"Colin?"

She frowned. "He was the CEO of the company. He was dashing and charismatic and had all the right traits to not only sweep me off my feet but to pull the wool over a lot of people's eyes."

Benjamin's gaze remained on her, an unreadable expression there. "Go on."

"He threw everything at winning me over. Flowers. Dinner. Jewelry. He was the most charming person I'd ever met, and part of me felt like he was too good to be true. Turns out, I was right."

"What happened?" The question was asked without judgment—only curiosity.

"He dated me mostly to distract me from asking any more questions. Of course, I didn't realize that at the time. Meanwhile, his company *was* dumping chemicals into a river and paying off county inspectors not to report it. Through the years, those chemicals caused cancer for some people in town."

Benjamin's eyes widened. "Wow."

"If I hadn't allowed myself to get distracted with romance, I could have kept asking questions. I could have told the proper authorities sooner and stopped it. But I fell for him. I fell for his story. I trusted him."

"You couldn't have known . . ."

"But that's the thing. My instincts made it clear something was wrong, and I didn't trust my own gut. That's on me." She tightened her arms over her chest.

Benjamin reached over and squeezed her hand. "I'm sorry, Lindsey. What happened?"

"It all came out what was going on, and, even though I was a whistleblower, I was made to look like a bad guy right along with the rest of them. I

began to get threats. Even though the police ultimately cleared me, people in the town still
hated me."

"Ouch. And Colin?"

"He's in jail right now, awaiting trial. Like I said, I
was cleared. But by association, I'm guilty in many
people's eyes."

"So that's why you came here?"

She frowned as she stared into the distance. "I
needed a fresh start. The whole situation just made
me realize I had some baggage of my own I needed
to deal with. I thought coming here would be a way
to get closure for my past so I could start a new life,
even though I'm not nearly so certain anymore."

"Do you think that what happened there has any
connection with what's happened since you came
here?"

She ran her hand through her hair and
shrugged. "I've thought of it. It's a possibility. But I
didn't tell anybody where I was going. That doesn't
mean they couldn't have found out somehow. And . .
." Her voice trailed as she contemplated how much
she wanted to say.

"And what?"

"There was a fingerprint found on that note
attached to the brick. I was going to tell you, but

then I'd have to explain everything, and I wasn't sure I was up for that."

"Whose fingerprint?"

"Leo's. Colin's son. Colin is ten years older than I am, and his son was eighteen. I only met him a couple of times. I'm not sure why he would send me a note telling me I needed to leave now while I could. It doesn't make any sense to me."

"Me either." A frown flickered at the edges of his mouth.

Lindsey glanced up at Benjamin, suddenly feeling self-conscious. "So now you know most of my life story. How about you? Why did you really decide to come back here to Hidden Shores?"

CHAPTER SIXTEEN

LINDSEY'S QUESTION echoed in Benjamin's ears. *Why did you really decide to come back here to Hidden Shores?*

His throat went dry as he tried to formulate his answer. He kept his arm around the back of the bench, still trying to look casual. But it was becoming harder.

"I tried to keep an ear open for any new developments with this place. As you know, Hidden Shores was a pivotal part of my upbringing." Bile rose in him at those words. He wished he could just tell her the whole truth. "I saw that ad you took out online, saying you were looking for a handyman for the inn, and I thought it would be a good opportunity for me to reconcile my past. Seems we both had the same idea."

"You haven't been back here since you left?" Lindsey turned her full attention on him. Her eyes glinted in the bright sunlight, and the pleasant lines of her face made her seem so innocent.

The woman was beautiful—but she wasn't the type to flaunt it.

Then again, he'd known she was beautiful from his memories of years ago.

He remembered her question and pressed his lips together momentarily before launching into his story. "No, I haven't been back here in more than a decade. After my dad was arrested, I went to live with my aunt. As soon as I graduated from high school, I joined the Navy. I put in ten years. Afterward, I moved around some before going back to Tennessee. I've done some other jobs since then. I just thought that coming back here would be a good change for me also."

Guilt pounded at Benjamin as he said the words. They weren't *all* a lie. But what he'd told her didn't form the complete picture.

"I can only imagine what you've been through." Lindsey pushed a lock of hair behind her ear as she offered a compassionate smile. "I feel like you must blame me for what happened to your dad."

Her words caused his heart to lurch. "Why would I blame you?"

"It's because of me that he went to jail," her words rushed out. "And he died while he was in jail. If he hadn't been arrested, then maybe he would have never had a heart attack."

"But you weren't the one who said he was guilty."

"I just felt like people needed a scapegoat and, for some reason, they picked your dad. He was always kind to me." Lindsey's chin trembled.

Benjamin rubbed the back of his neck, trying to retain control of his thoughts. "My dad was a kind man."

Her wide, imploring eyes met his. "Life just isn't fair sometimes, is it?"

He opened his mouth, desperately wanting to tell Lindsey everything. But he couldn't do that. Because every time he started to, he remembered Natalie. Remembered that she was the reason he was doing this job.

You're not the person I thought you were.

Those were the words Ashley had muttered to him when she'd broken up with him. Benjamin almost felt like he was living out a prophecy now.

And he didn't like himself for it.

Before he could say anything, Lindsey's phone beeped, and she looked down at it. Her face went pale as she read the message there.

Benjamin knew without a doubt that something was wrong.

LINDSEY COULDN'T DRAW her gaze away from her phone and the words she'd read there.

"What is it?" Benjamin leaned closer, concern in his voice.

She pulled her gaze up to meet his. She licked her lips before saying, "I just got a message from Allison, one of my old coworkers back in Staunton. She said Colin is out on bail."

Benjamin's eyes widened. "When did he get out?"

Lindsey read the message on her screen again. "A week ago, if I'm reading this correctly."

"Could he be behind what's happened here at the inn since you arrived?"

Lindsey sighed and tapped her lips in thought. "I can't believe Colin would set up his own son. Besides, Colin ran me out of town *and* he's facing prison time."

"But if he feels like you ruined him then maybe he wants revenge whatever the cost."

Lindsey let that thought sink in. Benjamin had a point. She didn't want to believe it could be true, but she didn't want to be naive either. "Do you think I should let Sheriff Ross know so he can keep his eyes open?"

Benjamin nearly snorted. "I don't think Sheriff Ross has any idea what he is doing. His eyes might be open, but I highly doubt he'll 'see' anything."

"You're probably right." Lindsey nibbled on her lip as she contemplated her options. "I don't know what to do. It seems like trouble is following me wherever I go."

He squeezed her hand again. Lindsey liked the feel of his fingers brushing against hers. She never thought she'd say something like that.

As a preteen, she hadn't felt anything toward Benjamin. Then again, she'd been so young. She didn't care about romance like some girls her age did. Could she have been wrong about him back then? Maybe he wasn't just a troublemaker.

"Whatever you need me to do, you just let me know," Benjamin's voice sounded hoarse with emotion. "I mean it."

"You were always there for me. I can't tell you how much that means to me."

A strange emotion crossed his gaze. But Lindsey had no idea what was behind it. She wasn't going to ask. Not right now.

Instead, she was going to finish drinking her water and remind herself to breathe.

CHAPTER SEVENTEEN

BENJAMIN SAID good night to Lindsey before heading back to his room. As he did, unrest jostled inside him.

He couldn't do this anymore. Not after hearing Lindsey's story and learning about everything she'd been through.

But it was more than just hearing her story. Seeing her heart had changed something inside him. He felt his resolve beginning to fade.

If Lindsey found out his real intentions . . . she'd never forgive him. That wasn't a burden he wanted to carry.

But he knew he'd deserve it.

Making sure the bedroom door was shut behind

him, he pulled out his phone and dialed Dawson's number. The man answered on the second ring.

"Did you find anything yet?" Dawson rushed.

Benjamin lowered himself on the edge of his bed. "No, I haven't. But that's not all I called about."

"Then what is it?"

His mind raced. If he backed out of this job, how would he get money for Natalie? The other jobs he'd taken barely paid enough for him to make rent. He wasn't a gambler and didn't believe in luck.

So how?

He didn't know. But he couldn't live with this deception any longer. He was losing sleep over the guilt he felt.

"I called to tell you that I'm not going to be able to do this job," he blurted before he changed his mind.

"I thought you needed the money." Dawson's voice came out biting and terse. "For your cousin."

Natalie's image flashed into his mind. "I do, but I'm going to have to find another way to get it."

"I know time is running out. You're not going to be able to find another job that will earn you so much money so quickly."

Benjamin bristled, not liking the controlling tone in the man's voice. It wasn't Dawson's job to make that call. It was Benjamin's choice, and he didn't like the man interfering.

"That's not your concern." Benjamin's voice sounded harder than it had earlier, more determined. "I'll figure something out."

"I'm afraid it's not that easy."

His muscles tightened even more. He wouldn't allow himself to believe the implications of what this guy was saying. Not yet.

Benjamin's back straightened as he sat on the edge of the bed. "What do you mean?"

"I need you for this job. No one else can do this but you. You can't get out of it."

"What do you mean I can't get out of it? I'm telling you, I'm not going to find the information you want. I'm out. This isn't your choice." Benjamin sliced his hand through the air, even though Dawson couldn't see him.

"Check your phone."

"Check my phone?" Benjamin repeated.

"Just do it."

Benjamin let out a breath before lowering the device from his ear and glancing at the screen. He looked at a new text message he'd just received. It was a photo.

A photo of his cousin with her backpack, talking to her friends at school.

"Why did you take a picture of Natalie?" Anger rushed through his veins.

"I've been keeping an eye on her."

Benjamin's hand fisted at his side. "I don't like the implications of what you're saying."

"You're not supposed to like the implications. But listen, and listen closely. I have someone stationed near her home watching her. At my word, he's going to grab her. Do you understand?"

The message was loud and clear.

If Benjamin didn't do what his man wanted, then Natalie was going to pay the price.

His heart pounded in his ears.

"This is dirty," he growled.

"I know, but unfortunately, sometimes you have to get dirty in order to get what you want. What I want is some answers. Don't let me down. In fact, my patience is running thin. I wasn't going to put you on a timetable. But I think I will now. You have a week or . . ."

Benjamin's breath caught as the man's threat dangled. "You wouldn't."

"I would. Don't test me. Don't bother to tell the police either. I have connections all over, and, if you do that, I'll find out. I'll grab Natalie before the police have a chance to show up. If I'm anything, I'm a man of my word."

Benjamin's heart pounded harder in his ears. He couldn't believe what he was hearing. How could this man sink so low?

The line went dead. He knew that Dawson had ended the call.

He'd never even met the man face-to-face. Benjamin couldn't say what he looked like or where he was from even. He'd simply signed a contract to do this job. It seemed like any other PI job he'd taken in the past.

But it clearly wasn't.

He gripped the phone harder.

What was he going to do now?

First things first—he needed to somehow warn his aunt to be on alert.

AS LINDSEY CONTINUED PAINTING the next morning, her mind continued to turn things over.

Specifically, she kept thinking about her conversation with Benjamin the day before. It had been surprisingly nice. It was amazing how comfortable she felt opening up to him. In fact, for the first time in a long time she felt a true connection.

But she'd already fallen for the wrong guy once. She'd vowed not to do that again.

Colin had led her on. But he'd had ulterior motives. In the end, she'd simply felt foolish. How could she have been so naive as to think that the man really liked her? But he'd known exactly what to do to get her to the point of distraction.

A knock sounded at the front door. She set her paintbrush down and stared at the foyer.

How had someone gotten past the gate? She was certain it was locked.

Apprehension crept up her spine, and she considered getting Benjamin.

However, criminals didn't usually knock. And it *was* daytime.

Instead, she brushed herself off before walking toward the front door. When she answered, she saw Irma Brickhouse standing there.

"Irma," Lindsey muttered, pushing a hair behind her ear. "I wasn't expecting to see you here."

The woman raised a Tupperware container in her hands. "I made my blueberry muffins. You used to always love those when you were a kid."

Lindsey took them from her outstretched arms. "Thank you. I really appreciate that."

"I thought you could use a housewarming gift. I'm just sorry it's a little later than I intended."

"No, it's okay. Really, it is."

As Irma remained at the door, Lindsey realized the woman was waiting for an invitation to come inside. She remembered all the work she had to do, but she pushed those thoughts aside. People first.

"Would you like to come in?" Lindsey extended her free hand behind her.

Irma's eyes lit. "I would love to." She stepped inside and glanced around before shaking her head. "It's so different yet so much the same. We used to have some really good times here, didn't we?"

Lindsey offered a soft smile. She wouldn't exactly call her time here good. But she didn't say that.

"Do you mind if I walk around a little bit? I've been curious about how this place has held up. But I didn't want to trespass."

"Of course. I'll give you a quick tour."

As they walked through the inn, Irma reminisced about the days of old. The parties Lindsey's parents had when they were between guests. Because, despite how stern her parents were with her, when they were with their friends they were like different people. They were *happy*.

The change never failed to knock the wind out of Lindsey's lungs. She often wondered if her parents had even wanted her. Then there were other times when her mom would kiss her when she tucked her in bed at night, and Lindsey would feel warm and loved.

However, in the months before her abduction, her parents had become even more withdrawn and sullen around her.

So much about her childhood still didn't make sense. She'd always blamed it on her abduction. But what if there was more to it than that?

As Lindsey and Irma finished touring the second floor, they came back downstairs and paused near the door. Lindsey didn't want to kick Irma out, but she had so much work to do and she wasn't in the mood to entertain.

"I have an idea." Irma clasped her hands in front of her.

"What's that?" Lindsey's throat tightened with dread.

"Let's have a supper club reunion."

As soon as the idea left Irma's lips, Lindsey tried

not to recoil. The last thing she wanted to do was to relive her past.

"I'm not sure that's a great idea," Lindsey muttered. "This place isn't really ready to host anything."

"Don't be silly. It's just perfect. Everyone could bring something just like old times. It would be so much fun. What do you say? You wouldn't have to organize it. I could do it for you."

Lindsey thought through her options. She still wanted to say no, but another part of her thought it could be interesting to have the old gang here.

Because there was part of her that wanted answers. If anyone had answers, it was probably someone in that group.

Irma stared at her, still waiting for a response.

Lindsey sucked on her bottom lip as she contemplated what to say.

———

CHAPTER EIGHTEEN

"YOU'RE HOSTING WHAT?" Benjamin repeated, certain he hadn't heard Lindsey correctly.

She leaned on the door frame of the kitchen, watching him as he patched part of the wall in the kitchen after the electrical work there was complete. The windows were open, and a gentle autumn breeze drifted inside.

The fresh air added a crispness to the room and gave him a burst of energy.

But Lindsey's words had nearly knocked the breath from his lungs.

Lindsey shrugged. "I didn't know how to tell Irma no. She seemed so excited, almost like a supper club reunion would bring some healing to people."

"So, you said yes?"

"I *almost* said no. But I also figured that someone in that group could have some answers for me. I suppose I had ulterior motives."

He sucked in a quick breath. He hadn't realized Lindsey was this determined to find answers or that she'd go to these lengths. He wasn't sure whether to be scared for her or impressed.

"When is this taking place?" he asked.

"In three nights."

Benjamin paused from spackling the wall and took a long sip of his water. "Who exactly is part of the supper club?"

Lindsey shifted, her gaze narrowing. "Well, obviously Irma. Also, Fred who owns the hardware store in town—"

"I met him."

"He's an interesting guy, and my dad always liked him. They would talk about cars a lot. Anyway, the mayor was a part of it also, and Sheriff Ross."

Benjamin raised his eyebrows. "Sheriff Ross? Your parents were friends with him?"

Lindsey shrugged. "I never got the impression that they were really friends. I just think he somehow got to be a part of the supper club group."

"So, is this the good old boys club that Howie mentioned? The one that called all the shots?"

Benjamin climbed the stepladder so he could continue working on the wall.

"My parents didn't have any power here in town, if that's what you're asking. Their little supper club had nothing to do with that. If you're looking for the group of people who always called the shots, then you can look at the sheriff, Mayor Sorento—"

"Is he still the mayor?"

She shrugged. "I think so. Then there's Mrs. Whitley. She's one of the wealthiest women in the county. There were a few other people too, if I remember correctly. But I couldn't tell you their names."

"Very interesting." He shrugged as he continued to work. "It's your house and your choice. But it sounds like this party will be very interesting."

"I think it will be." Lindsey sucked in a breath and straightened. "I guess I should get back to work."

Benjamin's breath caught. An idea had been percolating in his mind all day—ever since his phone call with Dawson. He'd wrestled with how to handle it and had only come up with one solution.

"Actually, before you go, there's something I wanted to run past you," he said.

"What's that?"

Benjamin licked his lips, not really wanting to dive into this subject. But it looked like he didn't have much choice. Dawson had made sure of that.

He prayed he knew what he was doing.

But he felt less and less as if he did.

LINDSEY WAITED to hear what Benjamin had to say.

He climbed down the ladder and stood in front of her. "It seems like you and I are both at a stopping point. In fact, I need to wait until Howie returns before I work on any more of this wiring. He had to run into town to pick up some more supplies. In the meantime, I wondered if you might want to do a little scavenger hunt."

"Scavenger hunt?" Lindsey had no idea what he was talking about.

"I keep thinking about that trunk."

As soon as Benjamin mentioned the trunk, Lindsey instinctively reached for the skeleton keys around her neck. "What about it?"

"It *has* to have something to do with what happened when you went missing."

"You really think so?" She stared up at him, blinking as she processed his idea.

Benjamin narrowed his eyes, his mind clearly racing. "I mean, isn't it weird that it just happened to be outside that night? Then it was never mentioned after that?"

Lindsey shrugged. She'd thought about that fact before. "I guess it is a little strange."

"What if it's in this inn somewhere?"

She sucked in a quick breath. She'd never really thought about that. She just assumed it was gone.

"Do you really think that trunk is still here?" she asked. "What if someone found it back then? Or maybe my parents took it."

"Where are their things?"

She leaned back against the wall as she rewound her thoughts until they reached that time in her life. "I went through most of my parents' things after they passed, and I sold the majority of them. They didn't really have much of any value. They definitely didn't have a trunk."

"So where could it be?" Benjamin stared at her, an intense look in his gaze.

Lindsey shrugged. "I guess I never really thought about it. But you and I have been through this place. Don't you think we would have seen it?"

"We've been through *most* of the inn. But we've never really looked for it. I thought it could just be something fun to do. We've both been working hard. I know how much it means to you that you recover your memories."

Lindsey stared at him another moment, surprised at his suggestion. Was there more to this idea than he was letting on?

She couldn't possibly see why that would be the case. Maybe this was the Benjamin she used to know. The one with the crazy ideas—like sneaking outside in the middle of the night to see the glowing water.

Besides, maybe looking for that trunk would be a good distraction.

Finally, she nodded. "Do you know what? That actually sounds kind of fun. My wrist is getting pretty sore from painting anyway. So, let's do it."

Benjamin grinned. "If you find it first, I'll buy you dinner."

"And if you find it first? Does that mean I owe you dinner?"

"I won't force your hand. But I definitely wouldn't turn down dinner either."

She grinned, liking the idea of having dinner with him—even though they had dinner together all the time. Still, something about the way Benjamin said the words indicated this dinner might be a little more meaningful than the ones they usually shared.

Either way, Lindsey shouldn't read too much into it. And, either way, it looked like they were having dinner together.

Her gaze caught with Benjamin's, and she nodded toward the stairway in the entry. "Let's go see what we can dig up."

CHAPTER NINETEEN

BENJAMIN FELT SLIMY, and he didn't like the sick feeling in his gut. He'd wrestled with what to do all night and all morning. He finally figured out he'd just have to continue with his original plan.

He'd do anything to keep Natalie safe. But he also needed to protect Lindsey. Maybe being here with her was the best way to do that.

Still, he knew Lindsey would never forgive him when she found out the whole truth. He wished he could tell her everything. But Benjamin knew, if he did that, Natalie would be kidnapped.

He and Lindsey climbed to the second floor and found the attic access. He'd briefly gone into the space when he was looking at the electric wires. But the whole place was impossibly dark and dusty.

He grabbed a cord and pulled down the stairs leading to the attic. As he did, a musty odor floated out from the enclosed space.

"Are you sure you want to do this?" Benjamin turned to Lindsey and asked.

"Let's do it. Let's see what kind of secrets this old building might hold."

Benjamin knew he'd encouraged Lindsey to try to remember those forgotten days earlier. But he also knew that, depending on what type of secrets surfaced, they could create a whole different set of problems.

What was in that trunk that made Dawson desperate enough to threaten lives in order to find it? Whatever it was, it must be incriminating. That theory was the only thing that made sense.

Last night as he'd lain in bed unable to sleep, Benjamin had looked up Dawson Smith online. But Benjamin hadn't discovered anything about the man. Dawson was practically a ghost. He had no social media accounts. No mentions in the white pages. Nothing.

That only made Benjamin feel even more cautious about each new turn of events.

Shoving those thoughts aside, Benjamin turned to the pull-down steps. "Let me check this out first."

He started up the rickety rungs, testing them to make sure they were still solid. Each one appeared to be.

"Come on up." He reached down for Lindsey's hand, holding a flashlight in his other hand.

She cautiously climbed up the ladder. At the top, she slipped her fingers into Benjamin's, and he pulled her the rest of the way up.

Once she had her footing, the two of them stood there, surveying the boxes and old furniture stored in the massive space. Lifetimes of stories rested between these walls.

"The trunk might be a little hard to find in all this." Lindsey frowned as if overwhelmed at the prospect.

"At least it's not something small like a key." He nodded to her necklace.

"True. But we have a lot to unwrap." As she took a step back, she hit a cobweb, and the strands clung to her.

She waved her hands, suddenly feeling creeped out.

"Hold on, hold on." Benjamin stepped toward her and picked the webs from her hair.

"You didn't see any spiders, did you?" she asked.

His lip tugged up as he fought a grin. "No spiders."

"Since this was your idea, you're officially on patrol for the little critters."

"It's a deal."

Together, they walked around the space, peering under the sheets. Lindsey held the flashlight while Benjamin investigated each piece of furniture.

"So, tell me more about the keys you're wearing." Benjamin nodded toward her necklace. "Where do you find them all?"

Lindsey seemed to instinctively reach for the chain at her neck. "Wherever I go I look for them. But I usually find them at antique shops."

"How do you pick which ones you buy?"

"I look for the ones that look the most well-used."

"Why is that?"

Lindsey shrugged as they paced around the perimeter of the attic, heading toward the next corner. "I figured since they've been used more that they're more valuable. People don't usually lock things away unless they're important."

"Or unless they want something to remain hidden." Benjamin said the words quietly, almost as if he didn't want to bring it up, but how could he not?

"Or that." Lindsey frowned. "But I like to think that each of these keys held importance at one time. Significance."

"How many do you have?"

"I haven't counted, but more than a hundred."

He raised his eyebrows. "Wow. Impressive."

"I don't know about that. It's an odd thing to collect. I have a jar where I display them all. I look at them and think about all the secrets these keys could unlock."

He smiled. "I like that."

They moved toward a closet in the corner, and Benjamin tugged at the door. With a hard yank, it opened.

"Wonder what's inside there?" Lindsey muttered as she peered closer.

As she did, she paled and suddenly lost her balance.

Benjamin grabbed her elbow to steady her.

What had she seen that he didn't?

MEMORIES BOMBARDED Lindsey until everything else around her disappeared.

The dusty, wood scent of the closet tried to
sweep her back in time. Back to a place she didn't
know existed. That she wasn't even sure she'd ever
visited.

At once, she remembered overwhelming darkness. Cold, undefeatable fear. Indiscernible, urgent
voices.

"Lindsey?" Someone shook her.

She startled, and a cry escaped from her lips.

"Lindsey? Are you okay?"

Her eyelids fluttered until Benjamin's face came
into focus. In an instant, the memory that had
started to form disappeared.

She sucked in a deep breath as if coming up for
air. Then she staggered backward.

Benjamin grabbed an old wooden chair and
placed it behind her. "Maybe you should sit."

Lindsey didn't argue as the seat hit her knees,
and she nearly toppled into the ladderback.

Benjamin knelt in front of her, his eyes brimming with concern. "Take a few deep breaths."

She did as he instructed and let air fill her lungs
before slowly releasing it. She repeated the process

several times until she felt like she could breathe normally again.

Benjamin stared at her another moment before asking in a calm, even tone, "What happened?"

Lindsey ran a hand across her forehead, her head starting to spin again. She sucked in a few more slow breaths before answering. "I started to remember."

His eyes widened with realization. "Remember your abduction?"

"I guess. There was something about the closet, about the scent . . ." At the thought, her stomach churned until she feared she could throw up. She tried to concentrate on her breathing instead, tried to calm the panic that wanted to claim her.

"I've heard smells can trigger memories, that it's a more powerful sense than most people realize."

"I can understand that."

"What did you remember?"

She pressed her eyes shut as the images replayed in her mind. "It's . . . well, it's not much. But it was something, you know? I'm not used to remembering anything. But I was in a dark room. I could hear people talking. I was cold and afraid."

"That's it?"

She nodded again. "I know it doesn't sound like much—"

He squeezed her hand. "No, that's not it at all. It's not a small thing. That's amazing that you had a flashback after all these years."

Suddenly, shivers overtook her. Nothing she did seemed to help calm her anxiety. Instead of retreating from it, she knew she needed to ask questions, to talk this out. "Do you think I was kept in that closet? What if I was being held inside this inn the entire time?"

Benjamin swallowed hard enough that Lindsey saw his throat tighten. "I don't know. Do you want me to look inside and tell you what I see?"

Lindsey only thought about it a moment before nodding. "Yes, I need to know."

CHAPTER TWENTY

BENJAMIN'S HEART pounded in his ears as he stepped toward the closet.

He'd never expected this. Never expected that coming up here would uncover memories—painful memories—for Lindsey. He wouldn't have suggested it if he'd known.

Nerves raked through him as he gripped the door handle.

What would he find inside? Part of him hoped it might be where Lindsey *had* been kept. It would provide her with some answers. But on the other hand, it could also uncover trauma—a lot of trauma.

He shone the flashlight on the closet and opened the door wider. Most attics didn't have closets, did they?

Not in his experience, at least. Was this a later addition to the attic? Was it built just to hide away people who needed to disappear for a while?

If that was the case, the facts would implicate Lindsey's parents had been responsible for her disappearance.

Why would parents want their own child to disappear? It didn't make any sense.

Benjamin swallowed hard before shining the light inside.

But instead of seeing an old blanket or bed or pillows—evidence that someone had been kept here —neatly stacked rows of boxes greeted him.

He stepped deeper into the space to see if anything else might indicate Lindsey had been locked in here. He had to assume that many closed-in spaces smelled the same way. There wasn't necessarily anything distinct about this space that would give it its own unique scent.

Benjamin shined his light on the wall as he remembered the words written in the closet downstairs.

I didn't mean to do it. Please, forgive me. I beg you. Please!

Were there messages on this wall also?

He glanced at the slats there. All that stared back

at him were the wooden boards comprising the space.

He bit back a frown. He and Lindsey could go through these boxes, but he wasn't sure exactly what they'd find inside. He hoped it wouldn't be something that brought her more pain.

"Anything?" Lindsey's soft, fragile voice cut through the silence.

He stepped out and offered a frown. "I'm sorry. Just boxes."

Her entire face seemed to fall, almost as if she'd been hoping there would be answers there—answers that might provide a touch of hope. He hated to disappoint her.

Lindsey's hand went to her throat as she turned her troubled gaze on him. "What's in the boxes?"

"Let me open one and find out." Benjamin turned back toward them.

None of the boxes were that big. Maybe twelve-by-twelve, give or take a couple of inches.

Propping his flashlight on a shelf, he popped one of the boxes open. Old candles were stacked inside.

The next box held Christmas decorations, ornaments mostly.

The rest of the boxes didn't yield anything else new or exciting either.

He stepped out to share the news.

"There was nothing, was there?" Lindsey's voice sounded dull as if she'd prepped herself not to be surprised.

He slowly shook his head, almost hating to break the news to her. "No, I'm sorry."

She rubbed her arms as if chilled, even though the attic was rather stuffy. "So maybe after I was abducted, I was kept in a closet of some sort. Not necessarily here. Then again, we don't know when those boxes were placed there. Were there dates on any of them?"

"I didn't look. Let me double check."

"My mom always liked to put dates on boxes. She loved being organized."

Benjamin stepped back inside and turned the boxes around so he could see all the sides.

That's when a date caught his eye, one written in black marker. "Someone wrote December 29 on the side of this box."

"What year?"

Benjamin's gaze locked with hers. "The same year you disappeared."

Her face went paler. "But that would have been after I returned. Those boxes were put there right before we moved out of this place."

"There's one other thing I think you should know."

"What's that?"

He held up one of the boxes. "The handwriting on this box . . . to me, it seems to match the handwriting that we saw on the wall in the closet downstairs."

LINDSEY RUBBED HER NECK.

Her mom was the only one that made sense to have written on these boxes.

But if that was her mom's handwriting on these boxes . . . why would her mother have also written on the wall of that closet in the guest room?

Lindsey had never paid attention to her parents' handwriting before. It wasn't like her mom and dad had left her handwritten notes. At the most, she'd seen their signature on school papers.

This whole situation felt stranger and stranger—and more disturbing—by the moment.

"Maybe this has been too much." Benjamin's chest seemed to broaden as he blocked her from the contents of the closet. "We can go back downstairs. I should have never suggested—"

Lindsey shook her head. She'd taken the easy way out for too long. Only it hadn't been the easy way. Choosing to ignore her problems instead of diving into them had caused other issues in her life. Fear of trusting people was right up at the top of that list.

"No," she stated. "I need to do this. Let's finish looking up here. I'll be okay."

The look Benjamin gave her made it clear he wasn't so sure about that. But instead of arguing, he nodded. "Whenever you're ready."

Lindsey forced herself to stand and draw in another deep breath. She wasn't a quitter. She wasn't going to let these ghosts from her past haunt her now. She definitely wasn't going to let them chain her down.

Since she and Benjamin had already checked that closet, they could check the wall on the other side of the attic and see if they could find any traces of the trunk that had appeared—and disappeared— on the night Lindsey was abducted.

But right now, she wanted something to distract her as they searched.

"Could I ask you a question?" She peered under another dusty sheet and turned to sneeze.

"Of course."

Lindsey paused and studied Benjamin's expression. "Have you ever been married? Engaged?"

Surprise flooded his gaze as he paced forward. "I've got to say, I wasn't expecting that one."

Heat rose on her cheeks. "If it's too nosy, you don't have to—"

"No, I don't mind. The truth of the matter is that I was engaged at one time, but we called things off. *She* called things off, to be more precise."

Lindsey's heart panged at the grief in his voice. "Who was she? I always wondered what kind of girl you would end up with."

"Her name was Ashley. We met when I was in the military. When I got out, her father wanted me to come work for his company. He sold and installed fences all throughout Tennessee. But he wanted me to work in the office as a project manager. I tried the position for a few months, and I was miserable. I wanted to do something hands-on. Ashley told me I'd never make enough money to support a family by doing that."

"Ouch." They continued to walk the perimeter of the room, peering under more sheets but finding nothing.

Benjamin nodded. "Ouch is right. She told me I

wasn't the man she thought I was, and she ended things."

"I'm sorry."

He shrugged. "How about you? You ever come close to getting married? Were you and that Colin guy serious?"

"Thank goodness, we weren't. In fact, we only dated six months, although sometimes it feels like years and years."

"I bet, considering everything that happened between you."

"I also dated someone before that, right after high school, but we were only together for a few months. I guess you could say I have trust issues."

"That's understandable."

Just then, a voice called from downstairs. "Hello? Anyone here?"

Benjamin and Lindsey exchanged a glance.

It was Howie.

It looked like their little scavenger hunt was over . . . for now.

CHAPTER TWENTY-ONE

AS BENJAMIN and Howie continued to work on the electric wires, Benjamin couldn't stop thinking about the time he'd spent with Lindsey since he arrived here. The more he got to know her, the more impressed he was.

The woman had certainly been through a lot, but she was determined to hold her head up. That took an incredible amount of strength.

He'd be lying if he denied his growing attraction to her. But Benjamin needed to nip those emotions in the bud. Trying to strike up a romantic relationship with her right now was a terrible idea on so many levels.

"I'm not finding this line." Howie released the wire in his hand as he stood on a ladder. "It sounds hollow behind the wall, and I'm not sure we're going to be able to fish this wire out. I hate to do it, but we may have to open this one up."

Benjamin stepped back and looked at the chipped burgundy plaster in front of him. They were working in Lindsey's parents' old room, which also served as their private living area, trying to attack the electric work there. Once they got done with the first floor, they'd move on to the second level. This project could take up to two weeks to complete, or more depending on what obstacles they ran into.

Benjamin glanced around the space, surprised at how small the room was. But this was where Lindsey's family had spent much of their time. It was a small apartment of sorts . . . only there was little room for anything other than the bed, dresser, and a small couch.

Howie pointed to an area where the wall was different from the rest. "It almost looks like there was an access here at one point that was plastered over."

"It does, doesn't it?" Benjamin frowned. "If we have to open it up, then let's just get it done."

"Alrighty then. Do you have the tools to tear this bad boy down or do I need to grab mine from the truck?"

"I have some. But I left them in the dining room. Let me grab them."

Benjamin found what they needed and then returned, ready to do some demolition. Tearing things apart was one of his favorite stress relievers— and he could stand to relieve some stress right now.

After spreading a tarp on the floor to protect it from damage and debris, he swung his sledge-hammer into the plaster and watched as it broke into pieces and crumbled to the tarp. He repeated the process until a four-by-four-foot section of the wall was removed.

Darkness stared back from the other side.

Darkness?

Howie seemed to realize it at the same time he did, and they both stepped closer to peer through the studs at what was on the other side.

Benjamin had expected to see another wall on the other side of this one. Instead, the space was indeed hollow. It had probably been used for storage at one time. But why had it been sealed?

"No wonder I couldn't fish out those lines," Howie muttered. "You know, you might want to show Lindsey this. She could probably expand this bedroom and make it bigger. No need to waste this space. My guess is that this space was closed off to cut down on energy bills, and someone made it a cubbyhole for storage instead."

"That's an idea," Benjamin said. "But let's take a little bit more down and see what we have to work with here first. It needs to come down either way."

He took the sledgehammer and continued to demolish the wall. Finally, the opening was big enough to step through.

As dust and plaster particles floated in the air around him, Benjamin pulled out his flashlight and shone it around the space.

What was this?

Based on the flowery golden wallpaper and the wooden floor that extended into the space, it looked as if someone had constructed a wall to permanently close off this eight-by-six-foot area.

"It's like a secret room . . ." Howie looked around with a touch of fascination in his voice.

"I guess so." It made no sense to Benjamin why someone would make their room smaller when the area was obviously short on space to begin with.

But as he shone his light into the back corner, his breath caught.

An old, dusty trunk rested there. The piece was probably four feet long and two feet deep.

Was this what he'd been looking for?

AS LINDSEY HEARD heavy footsteps coming toward her, she paused from painting the kitchen wall. Benjamin stepped into the room, a strange, unreadable look on his plaster-dusted face. Tension instantly threaded up her spine.

"I found something you're going to want to see," he murmured, an almost haunted look in his gaze.

Her heart pounded harder at his eerie words. "What is it?"

"I'd rather you see it than tell you."

She put her paintbrush down, wiped her hands on a cloth, and followed him. With every step, nerves raked through her. Finally, Benjamin paused by her parents' bedroom.

Her curiosity grew stronger.

She'd heard the commotion earlier and had seen Benjamin walking past with a sledgehammer. She had figured that something had come up while he and Howie were working, which was to be expected during the renovation process. She knew if an issue was too big, Benjamin would have asked her approval first.

She stepped into the space and saw a section of

the wall had been removed. Darkness blackened the other side of the recess.

She still had no idea why Benjamin looked so grim. What was she missing?

Benjamin turned toward her, his apprehension seeming to deepen. "Did you know that your parents' bedroom had a finished space behind the wall?"

Lindsey stepped farther inside the room, waving the dust from her face. "No, I didn't know that area was hidden there. The wall was already in place when we moved in."

Her parents had bought the inn when she was six, and she'd lived here until she was thirteen. Almost all her childhood memories were here.

Neither Benjamin nor Howie said anything.

"How big is it?" Lindsey was buying time, halfway dreading what she might find. Benjamin wouldn't look this tense if this was nothing.

"I'd say the space is about eight by six," Benjamin said. "Your parents could have certainly used the extra square feet, considering you guys used this for a living room as well."

"That's for sure. But I never even would have thought this was back here. I mean, why wasn't it utilized?"

"That's not all." Benjamin's cheek jumped, almost as if he held back a frown. "In fact, the space isn't even what I really wanted you to see."

Her heart raced. "Okay . . ."

He motioned again for her to follow, and Lindsey stepped through the opening in the plaster, staying near Benjamin. He held up a flashlight and shone it into the corner.

Her heart thumped harder as an object came into view.

"Is that . . . is that the trunk?" Her voice jumbled as she said the words.

"I can only guess."

She squinted as she processed the discovery. "But . . . this doesn't make sense. That wall was already up when my family lived here. This trunk has to be older than the one we're looking for, right?"

"Someone opened the wall up enough to slip this inside and then patched it again," Benjamin said. "The area that was patched . . . it was probably where the headboard used to be so no one ever saw it."

"Do you think my parents did that?" Her mind scrambled to put together the complete picture.

He shrugged. "Given the timeline . . . that's my best guess."

"So . . . my parents may have put this here?" She felt her throat tighten until she could hardly even swallow. "What's inside?"

"I didn't want to open it until you saw it first."

She gripped the skeleton keys at her neck. "I appreciate that. How about we bring it out here and see why someone went to all this trouble?"

CHAPTER TWENTY-TWO

LINDSEY STARED at the trunk after Benjamin and Howie had carried it into the center of the bedroom. The storage container was covered in dark hickory leather, outlined in rivets, and covered in dust. As they all gathered around it, she felt the anticipation in the air.

Benjamin tugged at the lid, but it didn't budge. "Do you want me to pry it open?"

"No, let's try one of these first." Lindsey slipped the necklace from around her and knelt on the floor.

She grabbed the first key, knowing it was a long-shot that one of these might fit. But she didn't know how complicated the lock was. If it was something simple, then maybe one of these keys might trigger the latch and open it.

It was worth a shot. She tried the first one but nothing. The same with the second and the third.

None of them worked.

"I have more," she murmured. "I can get them."

"Or we could just force it open," Howie said.

She shook her head, something deep inside urging her not to do that. "Then the trunk might be messed up beyond repair. Or maybe forcing it open would damage something inside."

She didn't know for sure. She just knew she wanted to try her keys first.

"You get the rest of the keys, and we'll wait," Benjamin said reassuringly.

She sent him a look of gratitude before hurrying to the room next door and grabbing the jar she kept on her dresser. Back in her parents' old room, she scattered the keys on the floor, grabbed one, and jammed it in the lock.

It didn't work.

Every time she tried one and it didn't work, she dropped it back into the jar.

Finally, she was down to the last ten.

"Prying it open would be a lot faster," Howie muttered, almost sounding annoyed.

"Look, if you need to go do some work at another part of the building, then feel free," Benjamin interjected. "But this is Lindsey's property, and she can do with it as she pleases."

Lindsey appreciated that Benjamin understood her and didn't pressure her to hurry this process. This moment could be important.

Finally, with the sixth key from the last, the lock clicked.

Her breath caught.

It worked. It had really worked.

With bated breath, Lindsey flipped the latch open. She and Benjamin exchanged a glance, one that held entire conversations without saying a single word.

This was it. This was the moment they might find some answers they'd needed all these years later. More than a decade, for that matter.

With trembling hands, Lindsey pushed the lid of the trunk up. The overwhelming stench of rot rose from the box, enough that bile rose in her stomach. Had a rat died inside?

Benjamin and Howie leaned in closer.

But an old quilt stared back.

Lindsey thought she remembered seeing that somewhere before here at the inn. The star pattern and bright red, yellow, and blue colors were distinct.

Her throat tightened.

What would be underneath it? What if it was nothing, just some old books and keepsakes of little importance to anyone other than the person who had saved them?

Or what if it was money?

Photos of her family?

Or what if . . . the trunk held answers concerning her abduction?

Her arms continued to tremble as she reached inside and pulled back the quilt.

A scream left her lungs when she saw what was beneath it.

IN ONE MOVE, Benjamin put his arms around Lindsey and turned her away from the trunk so she could no longer see what was inside.

Turned her so she couldn't see the *skeleton* inside.

A body had been crammed into the trunk. It had been there so long only a few scraps of flesh and clothing remained on the bones.

Howie muttered beneath his breath as he stood behind them. "Now *that* was unexpected."

Benjamin held Lindsey tighter, wondering if she

was having more flashbacks, if this had triggered more memories.

"I can't believe this . . ." Lindsey shook her head in disbelief. "Who is that? Who put him in there?"

"I'm afraid I can't tell you that. We'll have to call in law enforcement."

"The last thing I want is for Sheriff Ross to poke his nose into it," Lindsey murmured. "Besides, I'm not going to trust anything that man tells me."

"Maybe we can go over him," Benjamin said. "There's got to be someone we can talk to—someone we trust."

Lindsey pulled away from Benjamin and blinked several times. Then she cast a hesitant glance back at the trunk.

"How old do you think that body is?" Her voice came out barely above a whisper.

He stared at the skeleton and shrugged. "I really don't know. But pretty old, I'd guess based on the level of decomposition."

Lindsey's skin took on a sickly pallor as she continued to study their find. "Is there anything else in the trunk? Anything besides the skeleton and the quilt?"

Benjamin frowned at the thought of any more surprises. "There could be something at the bottom that we can't see. But we shouldn't move the skeleton. As much as we want to know, we could disturb evidence. We don't want to do that."

Lindsey continued to grip his arm as she stared into the trunk. "No, we don't. But we need to call somebody. Now."

CHAPTER TWENTY-THREE

THIRTY MINUTES LATER, State Police Officer Wally Williams arrived at the Hidden Shores Inn. Unfortunately, he brought Sheriff Ross with him.

Lindsey could have been imagining things, but she thought the sheriff scowled at them when he stepped inside. If she had to guess, the man didn't appreciate them calling the state police before him.

"What's this I hear about skeletal remains?" Officer Williams started.

The man appeared to be in his mid-thirties, with thick brown hair and a serious gaze. His stiff posture, combined with his measured words, already made Lindsey feel more confident about his abilities.

The five of them stood in the foyer to explain the situation.

"Things sure have been interesting since you came to town." Sheriff Ross narrowed his gaze as he studied Lindsey.

This time, Lindsey tried to hold back a scowl. "Follow me, and I'll show you where we found it. We didn't touch the skeleton, just so you know."

"That's good to hear." Officer Williams glanced around as they stepped from the foyer. "How old is this place?"

"More than a hundred years," Lindsey said. "My family used to run it when I was a child, and it closed down when we left."

"Interesting."

After leading them into the bedroom, Lindsey pointed to the trunk. Her throat tightened as she looked at it.

"Well, would you look at that." Officer Williams peered at the skeleton inside. "I've seen a lot of things in my years as a state officer, but never this."

"Can you tell anything about the body just from looking?" Benjamin asked.

"I'll leave that to the medical examiner." Officer Williams continued to stare at the skeleton with professional curiosity. "Let me take a few pictures, then I'll take the trunk with me so the medical examiner can look at these remains."

"Not so fast. This is my jurisdiction." Sheriff Ross turned toward the state police officer. "This *is* my town."

"This case is going to end up back with the state police anyway, so it might as well just start with us now." Officer Williams shrugged, unaffected by the territorial tone in Ross' voice.

"Maybe you should give your sergeant a call to double-check," Ross challenged.

As Lindsey listened to the two men go back and forth, she wondered if the sheriff had ulterior motives for wanting to keep the case in-house. There had always been something about the man that she didn't like.

It didn't mean Sheriff Ross was a killer or that he was involved in her abduction. But still, she just got a bad vibe from him.

Officer Williams pulled a camera from his bag and began taking pictures. "I don't need to call anyone above me. But you're welcome to if that makes you feel better."

Sheriff Ross scowled. Instead of doing anything, he stood with his hands on his hips watching the officer work.

A few minutes later, Officer Williams slipped on some gloves, closed the trunk, and got the sheriff to help carry the trunk out to his car. Lindsey and Benjamin followed behind.

"How long do you think it will take to identify the bones?" she asked.

"Hard to say," Officer Williams told her. "It depends, at this point, if we can match the dental. The medical examiner may be able to determine the age of these bones and, if that's the case, we can see if there are any missing person reports dating back to that time. It probably won't be a fast process."

"Can you remember any missing persons in this area? Anything from several years ago?" Lindsey asked.

The sheriff shrugged. "The biggest thing that happened in this town was your abduction. Before that, it was a couple who were killed on the side of the road in a hit-and-run. Why do I remember those things? Because bad things rarely happen here. When they do, people don't forget."

Lindsey shivered. "No, I guess they don't."

"What about our work in that room?" Benjamin asked. "Can we continue?"

"You'll need to work on some other projects around the inn until we process the space," Williams said.

A few minutes later, Williams and Ross left.

Lindsey thought she'd feel better, but she didn't. Part of her wanted to keep that trunk and find answers. But she knew she wasn't equipped to analyze everything inside.

Still, she hoped that between Officer Williams and the medical examiner, one of them would find answers.

Because those answers might provide insight into her childhood—insight she needed in order to move on.

"WELL, I have to say, finding a hidden room with a hidden skeleton in it is a first for me," Howie said when Benjamin and Lindsey stepped back into the inn.

Neither of them said anything.

After a moment of silence, Howie finally shrugged, seeming to understand that neither were in the mood to talk to him right now.

"How about if I work on the north wing of the inn?" Howie offered. "No need to waste any time, right?"

"That sounds like a good idea," Benjamin said. "Thank you."

Howie grabbed his things and disappeared down the other wing.

Benjamin waited several minutes, sensing that Lindsey needed a moment to process what just happened. His own mind wouldn't stop racing.

More than anything, he'd wanted to look inside that trunk. To remove the bones. To see if he could find anything else in the confines of the container that might provide an answer that Dawson wanted. An answer that would get the man off his back.

Because right now, Benjamin felt stuck between a rock and a hard place.

He wanted out of this deal, but any way he looked at it, someone would get hurt. He hated that he was in this position, and he didn't know what he should do about it now.

Benjamin turned toward Lindsey. "How are you doing?"

She shrugged, her gaze still appearing glazed. "To be honest, I don't know. I'm definitely shaken. I know finding answers is going to take time, but I desperately want to know whose skeleton that was. How long it's been inside this inn. We saw that trunk outside the night I was abducted. I'm sure of it."

His shoulders tightened. "I know."

"Was that dead body already inside? Or was it

put inside afterward? Or . . . did that body belong to the person we saw hanging on the tree?"

Benjamin's throat tightened. "I don't know. To my knowledge, the police never looked into that allegation. No one believed us."

Lindsey frowned. "I know. But I've never forgotten the sight of it."

He squeezed her arm. "Calling the state police was a good idea. Hopefully, Officer Williams will be able to find some answers, and this will be over soon."

"Not if Sheriff Ross has anything to do with it." Lindsey pressed her lips together in a frown. "I had a bad feeling from that man."

"Me too." Benjamin felt his jaw tighten every time he thought about the sheriff. "I don't trust him to work with the state police on this."

Lindsey turned toward him, her gaze sharp and curious. "What do you mean?"

"I mean, I know I'm not a detective." His throat burned as he said the words. "But it seems to me the sheriff might know something he's not sharing with anyone. I'll be keeping my eyes open until we know what's going on. Maybe I'll even ask a few questions around town."

"Asking questions around here just might land

you in hot water. That's how it seems right now, at least." Worry filled Lindsey's gaze as she stared up at him.

"I know what you're saying. But I just can't let this go. I want to know what's been happening too."

Lindsey squinted again, her gaze almost scrutinizing. "Why? Why does it matter to you so much?"

He knew he needed to answer very carefully. "I guess I'm a sucker for mysteries. It probably goes back to my days reading the Hardy Boys."

She flinched. "You read the Hardy Boys? Why don't I remember you ever mentioning that—especially since I loved Nancy Drew so much?"

He swallowed hard again, hoping he wasn't digging himself into a hole. "I don't know. Why *don't* you remember that?"

Her expression remained curious, not satisfied. "Next you're going to tell me you don't remember the time you talked me into sliding down the stair railing—except you didn't talk me through how to stop at the end. I hit that table and shattered my mom's favorite vase. I was grounded for two weeks."

He forced a smile. "Not one of the moments I'm very proud of. I tried to block those moments out."

She continued to stare at him. "Either way, is that really a reason to get involved? Just out of curiosity?"

"I also want this solved because you're involved." Benjamin's voice sounded hoarse. But his words were true. He knew Lindsey needed closure.

"Because of me?" She placed her hand over her heart as if surprised.

He lowered his voice. "Yes, because of you. You've taken on the gigantic task of restoring this place. And you need answers. If I'm capable of helping you find any, then I'd like to do that."

Lindsey stared at him another moment before finally nodding. "Okay, then. But don't get in trouble or get hurt on my account. Please. Because I'll never forgive myself if you do."

"Understood."

Benjamin hoped he could hold up his end of the bargain.

CHAPTER TWENTY-FOUR

LINDSEY AND BENJAMIN both turned in early that night. A long day of hard work had exhausted them.

But every time Lindsey drifted to sleep, nightmares about that skeleton haunted her thoughts. More than once, she'd woken up in a cold sweat.

Adding to that was the thunderstorm that raged outside. Thunder rumbled. Lightning flashed. Wind and rain pounded against the house.

As she fought to go back to sleep, her mind wavered from conscious thoughts to dreams until she didn't know which was which.

It's terrible what happened, the voice whispered to her.

Yes, it was terrible. What happened to her was

terrible. Whatever happened to the person in that trunk was terrible. In fact, life could be full of terrible things. Maybe it was what a person focused on that was important.

I tried to tell them, the same voice said, almost as if somebody narrated her dreams for her.

Lindsey's thoughts drifted back to her childhood. At once, she felt like a little girl again, sleeping in her same bed. Trying to rest as the guests in the lobby insisted on having a little too much fun together.

But she'd had school the next day, so she'd had no choice but to try to sleep.

Occasionally, her mom would come into the room to check on her. Sometimes, she would have kind words. But other times, if she noticed Lindsey was awake or that she had a book in the bed to read herself to sleep, her mom would scold her.

Right now, Lindsey could practically feel her mom brushing her hair away from her face and murmuring words of encouragement.

Her lungs tightened as something tried to get her attention. Why were there times she felt like her mom was right here beside her?

Her mom was dead. She'd been dead for more than five years.

The mind could play funny tricks on you, at one

moment making you relive your darkest fears and at the next moment teasing the desires of your heart.

As sleep seemed to swirl around Lindsey, she again felt her mom brushing her hair back from her face.

It's terrible what happened to you, the same soft voice whispered again.

Why did her mom keep saying that?

Only . . . it didn't really sound like her mom's voice.

At once, Lindsey froze.

If she was dreaming, then why did it feel so real? Why did she feel like her mom truly was sitting beside her, brushing her hair out of her face, and murmuring words of comfort in her ear?

Her heart pounded harder. *Get a grip, Lindsey. Get a grip.*

Something shifted on the bed beside her.

She hadn't dreamt that . . . had she?

Sickly sweat scattered across her forehead. What was happening right now?

It's a dream. Just a dream.

She squeezed her eyes shut and willed herself to fall into the deep depths of slumber again. When she woke up, maybe everything would feel normal.

She would laugh at herself for feeling so deeply over a mere dream.

But before she could drift to sleep—or even come close to it—she felt someone brushing her hair from her cheek again.

"I was going to come back for you, Lindsey," someone said. "But they wouldn't let me."

Lindsey's eyes flung open, and a scream flew from her lips.

BENJAMIN HEARD the scream and jumped out of bed. In five seconds flat, he'd pulled on some sweats and darted down the hallway.

That scream had come from Lindsey's bedroom.

Adrenaline pumped through his blood as he threw the door to her room open. He paused and glanced around.

A woman sat on Lindsey's bed, a white shawl wrapped over her head.

Lindsey had pulled her knees to her chest and curled herself into a ball on the other side of the bed. She stared at the figure.

Was it a ghost?

Benjamin didn't believe in ghosts.

He shook his head, trying to clear the cobwebs and think clearly.

Quickly, he reached over and flipped on the light.

As light filled the room, a frail-looking woman glanced up at him, her hollow gaze meeting his.

He halfway expected the woman to disappear as the darkness faded.

But that would mean she was a ghost.

This woman was clearly an actual person.

Finally, Benjamin came to his senses and realized who it was. "Irma?"

The woman shifted toward him. "I had to check on Lindsey. I've been so worried about her."

He glanced at Lindsey, who shrugged. She still looked shaken, but she'd come out of her state of shock some. That must have been a sight to wake up to.

Slowly, Lindsey loosened and lowered her knees, her shoulders softening. "How did you get in here, Irma?"

The woman didn't seem to hear her as she continued to talk. "It's terrible what happened. Just terrible. So, so terrible. You were just the sweetest girl."

Lindsey exchanged glances with Benjamin before leaning toward Irma. "Are you okay, Irma?"

"I'm just worried about you."

"I'm worried about *you*," Lindsey murmured. "We should probably get you home."

"I'm not sure that's a good idea." Benjamin's stomach tightened as he got a better idea of what was happening. Irma wasn't making any sense.

A wrinkle formed between Lindsey's brows. "What do you mean?"

"I'm not sure she's in her right mind right now. The last thing you want is for someone who's out of it to be home alone in a house located on a cliff by the water during a storm."

Realization rolled over Lindsey's features, and she nodded. "Who should we call? What should we do?"

"I hate to say it, but maybe we need to call the sheriff. Maybe he has some insight as to what's going on."

Lindsey stared at him another moment before nodding. "Good idea. Why don't you do that? Meanwhile, I'll get Irma some water."

CHAPTER TWENTY-FIVE

"IRMA HAS BOUTS OF DEMENTIA," Sheriff Ross said when he arrived twenty minutes later. He looked tired, like they'd pulled him out of bed. His hair was disheveled, bags hung beneath his eyes, and he kept yawning.

They'd all gathered in the living room. Irma sat on a couch on the other side of the room, Benjamin beside her. Meanwhile, Lindsey filled the sheriff in on what had happened.

Lindsey turned her gaze away from Irma and back to the sheriff. "She gave me quite a scare. I'm still not sure how she even got inside."

He pressed his lips together in thought and stared off into space. "I seem to remember that at one time she did have a key to this place. So, if you don't want people getting in, maybe consider changing your locks."

"I'll do that if I need to," Lindsey said. "But first I'd like to know for sure how she got in."

Lindsey glanced over at Irma again. The woman stared into the darkness on the other side of the window. Benjamin was a picture of patience and compassion as he assisted her. Seeing how well he handled her made Lindsey admire the man even more.

She pushed those thoughts aside and turned back to Sheriff Ross. "What are you going to do with her? Take her home? Benjamin and I were worried about what she might do if we left her alone at that place in this condition."

"She has a niece—Angela—over in Cape Charles. I'll see if I can take her there for the night. It'll be safer than anywhere around here."

"Good idea."

The sheriff's gaze narrowed as he studied Lindsey's face. "Did Irma say anything in particular?"

Lindsey's thoughts raced as she wondered exactly how much she should share. There was something she didn't completely trust about the sheriff, and part of her felt like the less he knew, the better. She couldn't exactly pinpoint why.

"She didn't say much," Lindsey finally said. "She just kept muttering that it was terrible what had happened. Just terrible."

The sheriff narrowed his eyes even more. "That's interesting. I suppose people with dementia tend to live in a different time in their minds. That's what I hear, at least."

"It's just so strange because every time I've spoken with her since I've been back, she seemed fine." Lindsey watched the sheriff's face for any sign of deception or any indication that he knew more than he was letting on.

His eyelid twitched ever so slightly. He *was* hiding something. But what?

"I hear she has spells," Sheriff Ross said. "It can happen sometimes during the beginning stages."

"I'm sorry to hear that. I always liked Irma." Lindsey had always thought the woman was a little strange, but she'd been kind.

"She's a good woman. But I'm not sure how much longer she's going to be able to live on her own." He let out a long breath. "Now, if you don't mind, I need to make a few phone calls to see if she can stay at Angela's place."

"Of course."

As the sheriff stepped away and put his phone to

his ear, Lindsey paced to Irma to see how she was doing. The woman offered a soft smile as Lindsey approached, but her gaze almost seemed empty.

"Such a lovely place, isn't it?" Irma glanced around. "I've always loved it here."

Lindsey sat on the couch beside her, her curiosity racing. "It *is* a lovely place. But it's terrible what happened, isn't it?"

Lindsey hadn't been sure if she should say it or not. But she wanted to know what the woman was talking about.

Was it a crazy delusion? Or was there more to the story?

And the bigger question was: did this woman know what had happened to Lindsey?

"I tried to stop him." Irma's gaze locked onto Lindsey's. "I did. But I couldn't. They wouldn't let me."

Lindsey's throat constricted. "Who is 'they'? What wouldn't *they* let you do?"

"They wouldn't let me stop the terrible thing."

"What terrible thing?" Benjamin leaned closer, clearly anxious to hear what she had to say.

Irma's gaze swerved back to Lindsey's and latched onto her. Tears pooled in her eyes. "Do you know what terrible thing?"

"When I was abducted?" Lindsey could hardly breathe as she waited to hear what Irma would say. "Is that what you're talking about?"

She waited, desperate for an answer.

Irma opened her mouth, but nothing came out.

"What is it?" Benjamin urged.

Irma pressed her lips together again, more tears pooling.

Lindsey continued to wait, hoping Irma might offer some answers to the questions haunting her.

As Irma opened her mouth again, Lindsey held her breath, bracing herself for whatever she had to say.

This could be it. The moment she'd been waiting for.

"Good news," a cheerful voice broke the moment.

Lindsey swerved her head toward Sheriff Ross as he sauntered into the room. His timing couldn't have been worse.

But as she glanced at Irma, she realized the woman had slipped back into a daze.

It was too late.

Whatever she was going to say was now gone.

"You can stay at Angela's place tonight. She's up and waiting for you now." Sheriff Ross reached down and took Irma's elbow. "Let me get her out of your hair and drop her off at Angela's. I'm sure you both would like to get some more sleep."

Lindsey's heart pounded. What had Irma been about to say? Had the sheriff cut her off on purpose? Or was Lindsey reading too much into this?

She didn't know. But something was definitely going on here.

BENJAMIN FELT his muscles winding tighter and tighter as the mystery surrounding this place deepened.

Beside him, Lindsey shivered as she glanced down the hallway at her bedroom door. "I just still can't believe that happened. I thought I was having a dream and then I opened my eyes and . . . there she was. I thought she was a ghost at first."

"I can't believe Irma got into this house without me hearing anything. Plus, I *know* I locked all the doors." Benjamin felt anger building inside himself—anger at himself. He should have been more alert for noises. At the same time, he thought he had secured the house.

"You're positive you checked *all* the doors? Even

the one leading off the kitchen?" Lindsey looked up at him with such hope and trust in her eyes.

He dreaded disappointing her, making her realize he wasn't the man she thought he was. As least for now, he could reassure her. "That's right. I suppose if Irma did have a key—as the sheriff suggested—that she could have come inside and locked the door behind her." Benjamin shrugged. "Hopefully, Sheriff Ross will think to check her pockets for those keys he mentioned."

Lindsey glanced around again, almost as if she expected another skeleton to jump out at her at any minute. "Sometimes I think I should just sell this place as it is and move on. Maybe me coming here was a stupid idea."

"It wasn't a stupid idea." Benjamin reached forward and squeezed her hand. "Sometimes you have to dig into your past in order to face your future. There's no shame in that."

Their gazes caught.

"You're a pretty smart guy sometimes," Lindsey murmured. "Nothing like the rascally guy you were when we were growing up."

He shrugged, trying not to show the guilt in his gaze. "What can I say? People change."

"I know, but sometimes it's like you're a whole different person."

More guilt pounded inside him.

Tell her, an internal voice urged him.

But another part of him—was it the cowardly side?—stopped the words from leaving his lips. Benjamin wasn't sure it was as much cowardice as it was uncertainty of the repercussions.

If he told Lindsey the truth right now, how would Dawson find out?

Most likely he wouldn't.

Unless Lindsey, in a fit of rage and anger, fired Benjamin from the job.

But he *had* found the trunk Dawson requested. What he couldn't figure out was why Dawson had wanted him to find the trunk. Had he known there was a body inside?

It didn't make sense. Benjamin would need to call the man later. He'd almost done it tonight, but he wanted to wait to see if the state police found anything else in the trunk first.

Still, as Benjamin gazed at Lindsey and realized his feelings for her were growing, he knew that, unless he came clean, any sort of relationship between the two of them would be doomed before it ever started. There was a good chance—a righteous chance—Lindsey would never forgive him for his deception.

At some point, the truth would come out. Benjamin knew that. But the sooner Lindsey learned his reason for coming here, the easier it might be.

Benjamin stepped closer, his throat burning with dread. If he had any kind of integrity, he had to tell her.

Now.

"Lindsey, there's something—"

Before he got his statement out, thunder boomed so loudly the entire inn sounded like it was tumbling around them. Lindsey jumped into his arms, her chest pressed against his. In that instant, their gazes caught.

He forgot about everything else except the look in her eyes. The curve of her cheek. The suppleness of her lips.

At least, he thought they were supple. He really wanted to find out.

"You were saying?" she said in a whisper.

He reached forward and raked his fingers through her hair. As he did, lightning flashed outside, filling the room with an electric-tinged air. The next instant, rain began pounding against the roof and walls.

A second set of storms must be moving through the area. The bad weather seemed like the perfect distraction.

Lindsey had taken him by surprise. Benjamin never expected to come here and run into the woman of his dreams. But that was exactly what had happened.

The next instant, he leaned forward and tentatively pressed his lips into hers. He waited to see if she felt the same thing he did.

As Lindsey practically melted into him, his hands circled her waist. He pulled her closer as the kiss deepened.

He was in trouble he realized. A lot of trouble.

On so many different levels.

CHAPTER TWENTY-SIX

LINDSEY COULDN'T BELIEVE she was kissing Benjamin. *Benjamin*.

If someone had told her this fifteen years ago, she would have laughed at the very idea. Hysterically. Maybe even rudely.

There was nothing about Benjamin she'd thought she would ever be attracted to.

Yet here she was, drinking in every inch of him. She just couldn't seem to get enough. There was just something about him . . . he captured her attention in every way.

Tonight had sealed the deal when she'd seen him talking to Irma on the couch and taking such good care of her in her vulnerable emotional state.

Benjamin was good at taking care of people—

including Lindsey. He'd been watching out for her since he came here.

She knew the man wasn't here to make money. She wasn't paying enough for any sensible contractor to do this job. But he was here because of *her*.

That fact hadn't gone unnoticed.

Now, as their kiss deepened, she wrapped her arms around his neck and enjoyed every moment of it. It didn't matter what he'd been about to tell her. All she wanted was to enjoy the moment.

Ever since she'd come here, it had been one stressful situation after another.

But not right now.

Right now, she felt like God had offered her a moment of joy in the middle of the storm going on around her.

He'd offered her Benjamin.

A few minutes later, Lindsey pulled away, knowing she needed to catch her breath. Knowing she needed to put some space between them.

But as they stood there staring at each other, both probably with goofy looks in their eyes, she let out a giggle.

"Are you laughing at that kiss?" Benjamin looked mockingly offended.

"I'm not laughing at the kiss. I'm laughing because . . . I feel happy."

He smiled softly. "I like hearing that."

"I wasn't going to say anything. But the truth is that you've been a real godsend, Benjamin. I'm so glad God brought you back into my life. Without you here for the past week . . . I don't know what I would have done."

Something changed in Benjamin's gaze, almost like a wall went up.

Lindsey wasn't sure what caused it. Had she been too forward?

She'd thought the two of them were on the same page. But maybe she shouldn't have rushed ahead. Maybe she should have waited to get a better read on the situation first.

Instead of ruining a perfectly good moment, she took a step back. "I think I need to go to bed."

He stepped back also. "Right now? There's something I need to tell—"

"Right now." She nodded quickly. "I'm exhausted, and we have a lot of work to do in the morning and . . . I just want the night to end with that kiss. I can't handle anything else right now, and I don't want to press my luck. Is that okay?"

"Of course."

She offered him another shy smile. "We can talk more later?"

"Definitely."

Before Benjamin could offer to walk her to her room, she hurried ahead of him. She rushed into her room and closed the door, locking it behind her.

But as soon as she turned and saw her covers, still thrown back in a fit of fear, she realized that, as much as she wanted to hang on to those good memories, the thoughts about Irma invading her space were going to be at the forefront of her mind.

And there was little Lindsey could do about that.

———

THE NEXT MORNING, Benjamin fluctuated between feeling on top of the world and like the scum of the earth.

He loved knowing he had a connection with Lindsey, yet he hated himself for not telling her the entire truth. Whenever he let his thoughts drift, he thought about that kiss he'd shared with her. He'd love to recreate it . . . over and over again.

If only life was that simple.

But it wasn't.

Before he left his room to grab his morning

coffee, he dialed Dawson's number again. But the man didn't answer, and the phone told him that the voice mailbox was full.

Benjamin lowered his phone and frowned. Of course.

He fisted his hands as he sat on the edge of his bed. What now?

He had no choice but to wait until later. He didn't even have this man's address so it wasn't like he could leave and track Dawson down, even if that was what he wanted to do.

Instead, he called his cousin Natalie. He needed to know that she was okay.

She answered on the first ring. "Finn! I wasn't expecting you to call."

"I just wanted to check in on you and see how you're doing." He leaned back against his head-board, thankful he hadn't called too early.

"I'm about to leave for school so you called me just in time."

"How are you feeling?"

"I'm doing better," Natalie said. "Lots of doctors' appointments, but that's nothing new."

"Any updates on that procedure we talked about?"

"Not yet. But Mom is setting up a fundraising

page. Maybe we'll get some money that way."

Benjamin frowned, knowing how hit-or-miss that could be. "I bet you will get some money that way. We just need to give it some time."

"By the way, thanks for the postcard."

His spine tightened. "The postcard?"

"Finn . . . stop being silly. You know you sent me a postcard with that picture of the sunset on the Chesapeake Bay. You asked me to come visit you . . ."

His head began to feel like it was spinning. But he didn't want to concern Natalie. "I would love to see you soon."

"When are you coming back?"

He let out a long breath. "This job could take another couple of months. But I hope to get back for a visit before that."

"I hope you can. I miss you, cuz."

"I miss you too. You take care of yourself."

That postcard was no coincidence. Someone wanted to make a statement.

Dawson wanted to make a statement.

More like a threat.

CHAPTER TWENTY-SEVEN

AFTER LINDSEY GOT SOME COFFEE, she sat down at the dining room table and stared at her phone. She'd like to say she slept like a baby last night, but she hadn't. She'd continually woken up in a cold sweat as she remembered Irma sitting on the edge of her bed.

Thankfully, her neighbor hadn't appeared again.

But last night's lack of sleep was going to require a lot of coffee today.

The good thing that had come out of last night was the kiss she'd shared with Benjamin. It had been so unexpected . . . but so nice.

She wasn't sure what it meant as far as things between them. But the two of them were still getting to know each other. So even though the kiss had been full of promise, she knew they needed to take it slowly.

Still, the prospect of things going deeper between the two of them secretly thrilled and terrified her.

After a moment of contemplation, she decided to call Sheriff Ross. She needed to know that Irma was okay. Wanted to know if he figured out how Irma had gotten into the inn.

Because if the woman hadn't had a key . . . then Lindsey needed to prioritize figuring out how the woman had gotten inside.

To Lindsey's surprise, the sheriff answered on the first ring.

"Good morning, Ms. Waters. How can I help you?"

He'd recognized her phone number . . . Lindsey stored that information at the back of her mind.

"I'm sorry to call so early," she began. "I just wanted to check on Irma."

"I took her to her niece's house. I haven't heard from them this morning, but Angela is a nurse. I really think that's where Irma needs to be full-time, but we can't force her to stay there. Not yet. But, rest assured, I think she's doing just fine."

That made Lindsey feel a little better. However,

she knew Irma loved living in the old carriage house. Decisions like this couldn't be easy. She hadn't had the chance to go through anything like this with her parents—nor would she ever. They'd passed away too young.

Lindsey's throat burned at the thought. "That's good to know. I have one more question for you, if you don't mind."

"What's that?"

"Did you happen to check Irma's keys to see if she had one to the inn?"

He let out a long breath. "She *did* have a single key in her pocket. I believe it might go to the inn. Next time I come by I'll check to make sure that's the case."

"That would make me feel better. I don't like thinking about people having a secret way of getting into the inn that I don't know about."

"Of course. I'll try to do that for you sometime today."

Lindsey ended the call with him and took another sip of her coffee. She was surprised Benjamin wasn't out of his room yet. He was usually up by now, but they'd had a very late night. Maybe he needed to get more sleep.

She still smiled when she thought about their

kiss. She knew part of her was more excited than she should be about seeing him.

He was so different from Colin . . .

Her throat tightened as she thought of her old boss. She didn't want to think about Colin, but how could she not? She'd fallen for him—and it had been a big mistake.

Before that, Lindsey had considered herself a discerning person. But how could she be discerning if she'd let herself be charmed by someone like that crook?

She remembered again that Colin was out on bail.

Could he have anything to do with the craziness happening here at the inn? She didn't think so. Especially not the trunk or Irma. Maybe the brick that had been thrown into her window could be attributed to Colin. Or the wires being cut or the text she'd received. But everything else didn't fit.

Still, Lindsey couldn't say with certainty that Colin was the type who'd come all the way here to teach her a lesson.

Once, his secretary had angered him after she'd botched his appointment calendar. He'd fired her and hired her best friend—and given the new secretary a raise, a fact that conveniently slipped out.

The man was vindictive, a fact she could clearly see now.

Colin was someone Lindsey needed to keep in the back of her mind.

As those thoughts raced through her head, her phone buzzed. She had a new text.

Her former coworker, Allison Stephens, had sent her a funny meme about coffee. On a whim, Lindsey picked up the phone and quickly called her.

After a few minutes of chitchat, she tried to delicately broach the subject of Colin. "I hate to ask this, but have you heard anything about him?"

"Well, I told you that he was out on bail," Allison said.

"Yes, but what's he been doing since then?"

"I ran into his brother the other day. He told me that Colin went out of town. Said he had some business he needed to take care of."

Lindsey's breath caught. "Is he allowed to do that since he's on bail?"

"Apparently, he just can't leave the state. Why?"

This little stretch of the Eastern Shore was still Virginia, even though it was a long way from Staunton.

She shivered again.

What if the business that Colin needed to take care of . . . was her?

JUST AS BENJAMIN walked into the kitchen and said hello to Lindsey, a knock sounded at the front door. During the day, when people were coming and going, they'd begun to leave the gate open, only closing it at night. Benjamin had walked out before meeting Lindsey to open it in advance of Howie coming.

He wasn't sure if he was relieved or disappointed his electrician had already arrived.

Part of him wanted another moment with Lindsey. He wanted to re-create their kiss last night—a kiss that had washed all his doubts away.

But as soon as the kiss ended, Benjamin remembered the secrets he was keeping from her. Secrets that he needed to share.

Instead of addressing the secrets head-on, it looked like he'd have more time to delay.

"It's probably Howie." He stepped back into the dining room. "I better answer."

"Of course." Lindsey nodded, almost a little too quickly.

It may have been Benjamin's imagination, but she sounded disappointed. Or maybe that was wishful thinking.

Benjamin let Howie in, and they walked to the south wing to begin working on the wiring again. The police hadn't cleared Lindsey's parents' old bedroom for them to continue their work in there yet.

He wasn't sure what kind of evidence the state police hoped they might find, but Benjamin knew there could be something in that hidden room—an old hair or fiber or fingerprint or *something* to indicate who had put that body in the trunk and then put the trunk inside the wall.

His mind had raced last night as he thought about it. Certainly, the scent of decay would have seeped through the walls when the body was fresh.

Wouldn't Lindsey have smelled it?

Unless she and her family had moved shortly after that body was placed there.

But even after she was abducted and returned, she'd still lived in this place for a few months, if Benjamin remembered all the details correctly.

There was still a lot that didn't make sense.

He and Howie chatted as they worked in the room. Once they got this done, Benjamin would need to work on the plumbing. Then he'd refinish the floors.

If Lindsey didn't fire him before then.

He had to tell her the truth. He just had to find the right time first.

An hour later, he and Howie moved into the next bedroom over. He noted the sheet that had been draped across one of the walls. He'd seen it earlier but hadn't thought much about it.

Why was that sheet there?

Out of curiosity, he pulled it down.

Charred wood greeted him.

He let out a breath. "There was a fire at this place?"

Howie glanced at it and shrugged, unaffected at the sight of it. "First I've heard of it. Then again, I'm not like some people in this town. I don't have to know every little thing that's going on."

"I understand. It does seem strange, doesn't it? Lindsey's never mentioned a fire." His thoughts continued to race.

"What are you thinking?" Howie studied his face. "I can see the gears turning."

Benjamin continued to stare at the wall. "What if someone tried to set this place on fire so they could destroy that body behind the wall?"

"You think someone would go to those lengths?"

"If they feared the body being discovered? Yes, I do. They've obviously gotten away with it for a long time. They wouldn't want to be caught now."

Howie let out a doubtful grunt. "I guess you could be right. *Maybe*. But if it was me and I'd gotten away with it for that long, I wouldn't be tempting fate."

"Unless someone found out about the upcoming renovations." Benjamin's mind raced.

How could he find out the cause of this fire damage and how long ago it happened?

He wasn't sure.

But his best guess was that someone at one time had tried to destroy the evidence by catching this place on fire.

CHAPTER TWENTY-EIGHT

LINDSEY WAS HALFWAY through painting the dining room when the sheriff stopped by.

"I'm assuming you're here to test the key," Lindsey said in greeting.

"Among other things."

Her curiosity spiked. What else could he be doing here?

He held up the key. "First things first."

He stepped to the door and locked it. Then he slipped the key inside and twisted.

It worked. Irma had a key to this inn, and that's how she had gotten inside. How many other times had she been in this place in all the years it had been empty?

Lindsey supposed there hadn't been much

vandalism here so maybe it wasn't a big deal. Still, another part of her found it unnerving. Did anyone else have a key to the inn?

When the sheriff left, she'd ask Benjamin to run into town to get the supplies he needed to change these locks.

But the sheriff wasn't done here yet.

She stared at him, trying to read his expression. However, she had no idea what else was on his mind. "Did you have something else to tell me?"

"A couple of things. I told you we ran the fingerprint on that note that was wrapped around the brick, and it matched with Leo Berlinski."

Her breath caught. "That's right. Is there more?"

"We tracked this guy down, and it turns out he's been in Costa Rica surfing for the past month."

"Then how did his fingerprint get on that paper?"

The sheriff narrowed his eyes, almost as if the whole situation annoyed him. "That's a great question. Maybe somebody set him up. Or maybe it was someone close to him who just happened to have a piece of paper that this guy had touched before."

She shivered as Colin's image came into her mind again. "Good to know. But I don't suppose that brings us closer to finding any answers, does it?"

"Not really. But I do have one other thing that I thought you might want to know."

As the sheriff said the words, Benjamin stepped from the hallway. He wiped his hands as if he knew the sheriff was here to share some kind of news.

He paused at the edge of the room and crossed his arms as he listened.

"We were able to identify the remains that were found in that trunk," Sheriff Ross announced.

"Already?" Lindsey's voice sounded squeaky as she asked the question. "I thought it could take weeks."

"It can, and it usually does. But the medical examiner took a guess on how old those bones were. Based on that, we cross-referenced it with any missing persons in this area from that timeframe."

"If you don't mind me asking," Benjamin interrupted. "What exactly was that time period that you were working with?"

His gaze darkened. "Fifteen years ago."

Lindsey rubbed her throat. Right about the time that she had been abducted. When those two weeks of her life were missing from her memory.

"So, you matched the time with a missing person?" Lindsey clarified as she leaned against the wall to steady herself.

"Not exactly." Sheriff Ross frowned. "This wasn't actually a missing person. It's someone we thought left the area by his own free will. There were no missing persons reports filed because we all thought he'd simply moved on."

"What made you think to check him out now?" Lindsey asked.

"This man had some extensive dental work done. In fact, he had a cleft palate."

"I see." Lindsey leaned harder into the wall to steady herself.

As she did, Benjamin glanced over, almost looking like he wanted to hurry across the room and help her. But he didn't, and that was a good thing. She didn't want to make a big deal out of this.

"Who was it?" Benjamin stepped forward as if he couldn't restrain himself any longer.

"A man named Johnny Flora." The sheriff studied their faces. "Does that name sound familiar to you?"

Lindsey's eyes skimmed back and forth quickly in thought. "The name sounds vaguely familiar. Who is he?"

"He owned a computer store in town—sold used computers and fixed broken ones for people. But I think he may have been to the inn once or twice to eat with your family."

"Could you tell how he died?" Benjamin asked.

"That's where things get interesting." Sheriff Ross straightened. "Based on what the medical examiner can surmise . . . he was hanged."

THE SHERIFF'S words echoed in Benjamin's ears.

"This guy was hanged?" He repeated what the sheriff had said, just to make sure he hadn't misunderstood.

"That's what it looks like based on the marks on his neck bones."

"Just like the man I saw on the night I was abducted."

The sheriff raised his hand. "Now, let's not get ahead of ourselves."

She narrowed her eyes, obviously not appreciating being dismissed.

"Maybe you can answer this then," Lindsey continued, a new hardness to her voice. "Did this guy have a record?"

The sheriff shook his head. "I can't say he did. He was pretty quiet. Didn't cause much trouble."

"He just ran a computer shop?" Benjamin clarified.

"That's right. He didn't get much business around here, but he seemed to like it here."

"Was he local?" Benjamin continued.

"He moved here in his twenties. Lived alone. Not many friends."

"I see. I appreciate you sharing that information." Lindsey straightened as if trying to pull herself together.

"Of course. I knew you'd want to know."

"What happens next?" Lindsey continued.

"We've already located his next of kin—an aunt is his only living relative. She'd lost touch for so long that she just assumed he'd started a new life somewhere else. Now we'll launch an investigation into what happened to him."

"I'm glad to hear that."

The sheriff nodded slowly. "Anyway, I need to be running. My schedule is suddenly getting very full."

"I'll walk you out," Benjamin said.

Something flashed in the sheriff's gaze, but he remained quiet. He simply nodded and let Benjamin walk him toward the door.

Benjamin wanted to talk to the sheriff and ask a few more questions.

Because he still didn't trust this man. There was something about the man Benjamin couldn't put his finger on . . . but whatever it was bothered him.

The sheriff stepped into the sunlight outside and paced toward his car, which was parked at the front of the inn.

"You have something on your mind?" Sheriff Ross cut straight to the chase.

"As a matter of fact, I do. I'm curious. Were you in town on the night that Lindsey was abducted? I can't remember."

The sheriff turned to him, more unreadable emotions dancing in his gaze. "I'm not really sure why you're asking or what you're getting at. But, no, I wasn't. I was at my uncle's funeral, and I came back the next day."

Benjamin stored that information at the back of his mind.

So maybe the sheriff wasn't involved with Lindsey's abduction.

"I'm glad I have a moment alone with you," the sheriff said. "Because I've been meaning to ask you if you remember meeting me when you were younger."

Heat spread through his limbs. "Of course."

"I was the one who arrested your dad."

"I know."

"You could have some hard feelings toward me, I realize. Feelings that may taint how you see things now."

"I don't know about that." Benjamin felt himself bristling.

"The thing is . . . there's something about you that seems different."

His breath caught. "What are you saying?"

"I ran your plates."

His spine tightened even more. "And?"

"The vehicle is registered to you. But I just have this feeling you're not telling the truth about something."

"I'm sorry you feel that way."

The sheriff stepped closer. "I'm keeping an eye on you, Benjamin. Never forget that."

CHAPTER TWENTY-NINE

LINDSEY WAITED after Benjamin came back inside, waited to hear if he had anything else to say about the sheriff or why he had walked him outside. She felt sure he had a reason. But he didn't offer any information.

Instead, he paused in front of her. "Are you doing okay?"

She shrugged. "I guess I don't have any reason *not* to be doing okay, even though something in my subconscious is telling me I should be freaking out a little. Does that make any sense?"

He offered a compassionate frown. "This is a lot for anyone to process. But you don't have any memories of Johnny Flora, do you?"

"I don't. I vaguely remember some guy in his

twenties with dark hair and pale skin. He really never seemed like a threatening guy."

"Do you think that the same person who abducted you also killed Johnny?"

"I don't know. In fact, the more I learn, the more I realize I don't know anything. I'm more confused than ever."

"I'm sorry. I can only imagine the stress that you're going through."

She let out a long breath as if trying to collect her thoughts. "You know what? I think I'm going to go into town to that little coffee shop and get a latte. And maybe a danish. Maybe two danishes. I'm not sure right now."

"You should do that. Do you want me to go with you?"

Lindsey smiled softly and stepped closer. "Ordinarily, I'd say yes. But I know you're busy working, and maybe I could use some alone time. I'm still trying to process a lot."

"I understand." He squeezed her arm. "If you need anything, you let me know."

"I will."

A few minutes later, Lindsey had cleaned herself up and started down the road. It felt good to get away from the inn. Too many bad memories haunted the place.

She'd meant what she told Benjamin earlier. Sometimes she wondered if it was all a mistake to come back here. Everything seemed to be going wrong since she had.

But what would she do if she wasn't here? Find another marketing job?

That prospect didn't thrill her either.

Still, she was going to have to make some decisions soon.

Ten minutes later, she pulled up to the coffee shop. When she walked in, she spotted Maple. Just the person she wanted to see.

"Hey, there!" Maple grinned. "You liked the coffee enough to come back?"

"Of course. It was delicious. I'll have a latte—and a danish, please."

A few minutes later, Maple set her order on the counter and Lindsey paid. But Maple's gaze remained on Lindsey long enough that Lindsey knew there was something she wanted to say.

"Everything okay?" Lindsey asked, lingering close to the counter.

"I'm sorry." Maple waved a hand in front of her

as she smiled sheepishly. "It's that obvious, right? I was just thinking . . ."

"About what?"

She let out a breath. "I talked to my mom and mentioned you were back in town."

"Okay . . ." Lindsey had no idea where she was going with this.

"She got all quiet when she heard. I thought it was weird."

"I don't even remember ever meeting her."

"I know. It's strange, though, because my mom had knee replacement surgery a year or so ago and I went to help her during recovery. Some of the pain medication made her a little loopy."

Lindsey continued to wait with anticipation.

"She started talking about how she left town because someone found out she'd stolen some money from her job," Maple continued. "I thought she was just talking crazy. But the more I thought about it, the more I wondered if it was true."

"Why's that?"

"Because we left so suddenly. It didn't make sense." Maple scrunched her lips together in a frown before beginning to straighten the stir sticks and sugar packets on the counter.

"I can understand that, but I'm not sure what this has to do with me . . ."

Maple paused for long enough to lock gazes with Lindsey. "When she was in that delirious state . . . talking about leaving and the money . . . she mentioned your name."

BENJAMIN HAD SEEN Lindsey come back from her coffee outing. But, instead of stopping to talk, she'd gone straight to work, only raising her paper cup to Benjamin in acknowledgement before getting busy.

Meanwhile, he and Howie had made good progress today and finished rewiring the first floor. Howie had been his usual talking machine, telling stories about his childhood. He'd apparently spent a lot of time sitting with his grandfather while his grandfather was ill. He relayed those stories to Benjamin now.

As usual, Howie left strictly at five o'clock. It was almost like a mental timer went off when it was time for him to go home for the day.

After he was gone, Benjamin made sure Lindsey wasn't around before grabbing his phone and trying

Dawson's number one more time. Again, the man didn't answer, and the call ended with a full voice mailbox again.

Benjamin's stomach churned harder. Without talking to Dawson, it would be hard to get any resolution. He didn't like the direction this was going.

As he put his phone away, he glanced down the hallway toward the dining area where Lindsey painted the walls.

Lindsey . . . a woman he was quickly developing feelings for.

She'd started to trust him, and that meant the world to him.

The last thing he wanted to do was hurt her.

He drew in a deep breath.

Benjamin had to tell her the truth.

He couldn't put it off any longer.

He was an adult. He would have to deal with the consequences.

But he couldn't wait any longer to tell Lindsey that his name wasn't really Benjamin.

CHAPTER THIRTY

AS BENJAMIN STEPPED into the formal living room where Lindsey painted, she turned to him.

She'd let him know she was back from the coffeehouse. But then her gaze had fallen on Howie, and she'd simply moved on to continue working.

"Hey, you," he started.

"Hey." Lindsey climbed down from her ladder and set her paintbrush down on a paint can there. "I'm glad you found me. I was hoping we could talk."

He observed her, with the flecks of paint in her hair and a few smudges of dirt across her cheek. Her T-shirt and old jeans also had paint on them, proving that she didn't mind getting dirty.

To him, she'd never looked more beautiful.

He leaned against the wall as he observed her,

feeling his affection for the woman growing with every day he got to know her better.

"What's going on?" he asked.

She paused in front of him and gave him a recap of her conversation with Maple.

He rubbed his chin, letting this new revelation sink in. "You have no idea what that means? Why Maple's mom would have said your name?"

"No idea. But isn't it strange? What's going on here, Benjamin?"

"I wish I knew. But it is strange. And multilayered, it seems."

"I agree." She shook her head. "I'm feeling more and more unsettled all the time, like I don't know whom I can trust anymore."

Benjamin's neck visibly tightened. "There's something I need to talk to you about also."

"Do you feel like telling me as we walk? Since Howie's gone for the day, I thought I would go ahead and close the gate. It gives me a little bit of peace of mind when we're here—not that it seems to have stopped anybody in the past."

"Sure." Maybe strolling together in the sunlight would make this somehow easier. Or maybe Lindsey would tell him to keep walking. To forget about his things and to go hitch a ride and that she never wanted to see him again.

That was a good possibility.

Benjamin slipped his hands into his pockets as they stepped onto the porch and down the stairs. The autumn breeze greeted them, and the sun warmed their shoulders. Leaves, rebelliously drying early for winter, scratched across the gravel lane.

Lindsey looped her arm through his as they headed toward the gate. The feeling of her close to him . . . it felt right. Like something he wanted to experience now. Maybe even for longer—for a lot longer.

"So, what is it that you wanted to tell me about?"

Dread pooled in his stomach. "This isn't going to be easy to say."

"Are you kidding me? Do you realize everything I've heard people say this week? If I can handle those things, I'm sure I can handle whatever you have to say also."

"It's about our childhood . . ." He was certain Lindsey had no idea the impact of what he was about to share.

She paused and turned toward him, heaviness filling her gaze. "You're still upset with me, aren't you? You blame me for your dad going to jail?"

He sucked in a breath. He hadn't expected that. "No, it's not that—"

"When I heard that he died in jail, I cried myself to sleep for weeks. Your dad was always such a nice man."

"Nobody blames you for that, Lindsey. Don't feel bad. You have no reason to."

She didn't seem to hear him as she stared off in the distance. "I feel like I ruined your life."

"No, you didn't." He grasped her arms, desperate to reach her. To tell her the truth. "That's not even possible."

Lindsey shrugged. "What do you mean? Of course it's possible. It's because of me—"

"Lindsey . . . no. It's not possible because I'm . . ." He swallowed hard, dreading this conversation even more now.

She stole a glance at him. "You're . . . ?"

He rubbed his jaw, hating the fact that he had to say what he was about to say. But he couldn't back out now. "Because I'm not—"

Before he finished, Lindsey grabbed his arm and pointed to something in the distance. She sucked in a quick breath before muttering, "Benjamin . . . do you see that?"

His breath caught as his gaze followed the line of her finger. He certainly did see something.

Two legs extended from beneath the brush. Unmoving. Unnaturally still.

"Who is that?" Lindsey's voice trembled.

"Stay here."

He stepped closer to see what was going on.

LINDSEY COULD HARDLY BREATHE AS she waited to see what Benjamin would find. But in her heart, she already knew the truth. She already knew what she was looking at.

There was a body. In the brush.

Based on the complete stillness of his legs, the man—the thick work boots signified his gender—was dead.

Part of her still hoped she was wrong. Hoped that Benjamin would appear and tell her that someone had just passed out on her property.

But she knew that wasn't going to be the case.

A few minutes later, Benjamin looked at her and frowned. "I'm sorry, Lindsey. We need to call the police."

She muffled a cry. "Who . . . ? What . . . ?"

"I don't recognize him. He looks to be in his late twenties, early thirties. He's dressed casually."

"And he's . . . dead?" The words seem to catch in her throat and nearly choke her.

Benjamin nodded somberly. "I don't see any blood. I wonder if somebody hit him over the head with something and then left him here to die. He's still warm."

"When would someone have done that? I just drove back up here a few hours ago. No one was here." Her arms trembled, and she rubbed them, willing them to still.

It didn't work.

"I don't know what to tell you. I'm completely confused by this just like you."

She noted the way that Benjamin stood in front of her, trying to block her from seeing too much.

"Let me call the cops." He pulled out his phone and dialed. After muttering a few things into the mouthpiece, he put his cell away and turned back to her. "Sheriff Ross is on his way . . . again. He said we should stay close, to keep an eye on the body . . . just in case."

She didn't say anything for several minutes. Instead, she tried to control her racing thoughts.

The task felt impossible.

She wasn't sure who initiated it—if she'd stepped closer or if Benjamin had. But she found herself nestled in his arms, relishing his strength as he held her up.

"What's going on here, Benjamin?" Lindsey buried her face in his chest as shock raced through her. "Why is this place shrouded in death and darkness? Maybe this inn isn't haunted with ghosts . . . but it's definitely haunted with something evil, if that makes sense."

Benjamin held her more tightly. "Unfortunately, it does. But I still believe it can be redeemed—just like people can be redeemed."

Her shallow breath slowed some. "I've always thought that. Even for myself."

"Listen . . ."

Just then, the sheriff pulled down the lane. He must have been close by to arrive this quickly.

It was just as well. Benjamin was probably going to try to reassure her.

But there was nothing anyone could say to make her feel better right now.

CHAPTER THIRTY-ONE

THE NEXT COUPLE of hours were a flurry of activity. Not only did the sheriff come but, several minutes later, ambulances and backup officers also arrived on the scene. Lights flashed in the distance. Officials gathered around the body. Eventually, the dead man was placed on a gurney and put into an ambulance.

Benjamin and Lindsey remained on the porch watching everything happen.

Benjamin remained quiet, hoping to hear snippets of conversation. As he did, he thought he heard a name drift through the air.

"Did you hear someone say a name?" Lindsey whispered.

"I think someone said Daniel Markson."

When Lindsey heard the name, she gasped. "What?"

Benjamin turned toward her. "You know him?"

"He was one of the people I called about working on the inn. He told me his schedule was full."

The sheriff joined them with a snort. "That boy has never worked a full day in his life." Then he straightened as if realizing the somberness of this situation. "I guess you overheard his name."

Benjamin nodded. "I did."

Sheriff Ross' gaze latched onto Lindsey's. "You never met Daniel in person?"

Lindsey backed away from Benjamin as if to compose herself. "No, never. I only talked to people on the phone before I came. I didn't meet anyone face-to-face."

"So Benjamin is the only worker you already knew?" The sheriff nodded toward him, but his gaze never left Lindsey.

Something about the way the sheriff said the words made Benjamin wonder if the sheriff had been looking into his background. What if this man learned the truth about him and told Lindsey before Benjamin had the chance to?

The thought of it made nausea roil in his stomach. Would the sheriff really be smart enough to figure out the truth?

Benjamin wasn't sure. But there was a chance the sheriff still thought Benjamin's father had abducted Lindsey. And in this man's mind, if Benjamin's father was a criminal, then there was a possibility Benjamin was a criminal also.

"Benjamin saw my ad online, and he showed up the same time I arrived here." Lindsey's voice sounded unwavering and sure. "The timing couldn't have been better. Right, Benjamin?"

He nodded, still feeling uneasy. More guilt flooded him when he realized how adamantly Lindsey was defending him—and, yet, here he was deceiving her.

"That's right." He forced the words out.

"How did you happen to see an ad for a handyman out here on the Eastern Shore when you were living . . ." The sheriff squinted. "Where did you say you were living again?"

More tension crept up Benjamin's spine. "Tennessee. I've always wanted to come back to this area. I was between jobs and looking for a change. Let's just say the timing worked out perfectly."

"I'd say so." A new edge entered the sheriff's voice.

"As soon as I realized the work was taking place at the old inn where I spent a couple years, I thought that this would be the perfect chance to get some closure on that period of my life."

The sheriff grunted before shifting his gaze from Benjamin to Lindsey then back to Benjamin. "I see. Convenient. Have either of you been alone for the past couple of hours?"

Lindsey and Benjamin exchanged a glance.

"We both have for periods of time," Lindsey finally said. "I've been working in the formal living room by myself."

"Howie and I were working in the other wing of the inn. We did split up for a little while, so I suppose we were both by ourselves for a short time."

"When did Howie leave?"

"Probably an hour ago," Benjamin said.

The sheriff nodded toward the area where the body had been found. "And neither of you have ever met that man?"

"No." Benjamin fought the defensiveness he felt rising in him. "Are you implying that we're suspects here?"

"Everything that's happened seems to have centered around the two of you. I'm just doing my due diligence." The sheriff's jaw twitched as if he were annoyed.

"Neither of us are responsible for this man's death." Lindsey raised her chin in defiance. "We didn't know this Daniel guy, and we have no reason to hurt him."

"Unless you suspected that he was the one responsible for these mishaps around the house. Maybe you wanted to put an end to that." The sheriff raised an eyebrow as his accusation remained suspended in the air.

"That's ridiculous." Anger heated Lindsey's voice. "Have the things happening here been annoying? Yes. Absolutely. But there's no way I'd hurt someone. Plus, I don't even know how that man died."

"We're guessing blunt force trauma." Sheriff Ross let out a long breath. "Anyway, you two are free to go inside for a while if you'd like. But we're going to be out here longer, searching these woods for any evidence that may have been left. We'll let you know if we have any more questions."

As the sheriff's narrowed gaze met Benjamin's, Benjamin swallowed hard. The sheriff was making it clear that he would keep an eye on him.

That was only going to spell trouble.

He needed to tell Lindsey the truth before she found out some other way.

But she seemed so stressed right now that he wasn't sure this would be the best time.

Maybe in the morning when she'd had a chance to calm down.

But he couldn't keep putting this off much longer.

———

"I CAN'T BELIEVE THIS," Lindsey muttered as soon as she and Benjamin slipped inside the inn and shut the door behind them.

She wasn't sure if this inn felt like her safe place or not. But right now, at least, it offered privacy from Sheriff Ross' prying gaze.

Benjamin pulled her into his arms and held her as they lingered in the foyer. There was nothing else he could say or do that might make her feel better. But a hug could go a long way. It was just what Lindsey needed.

"I can't believe this either," Benjamin murmured. "It seems like we stepped into the middle of a real-life thriller movie, doesn't it?"

"You can say that again. Sometimes I can't

imagine this can get any worse . . . and then it does." She continued to lean into Benjamin, relishing his strength.

After a few minutes, he stepped back just enough to look her in the eyes. "How about if you let me fix you something to eat? Maybe it will take your mind off everything."

Lindsey nibbled on her lip in thought. "Maybe. But I'm not really hungry."

"I make a really delicious egg drop soup. In high school, I worked at a Chinese restaurant, and egg drop soup became my specialty."

Lindsey offered a weak smile, knowing he'd sold her with his enthusiasm. "Some soup sounds good. If you make it, I'll eat it."

"Sounds like we have a plan."

The two of them walked into the kitchen together, and Lindsey sat at the kitchen table while Benjamin began pulling out the ingredients he needed.

But Lindsey's gaze continued to stray toward the windows. At any minute now, she halfway expected the sheriff to come back inside with more grizzly news of some sort.

Why would Daniel have been on her property? Who had killed him? And *why* had he been killed?

None of it made sense. Until Lindsey had more information, she supposed it wouldn't.

The man clearly wasn't old enough to have been involved with Lindsey's abduction. So, what was the connection?

Her mind raced through possibilities for the future. Maybe she could sell this place. She could move somewhere totally new. Just put her past behind her. Even though she'd already sunk a considerable portion of her savings into the renovations, sometimes it was just better to walk away and take a loss.

But what about Benjamin? Lindsey had agreed to pay him, and he'd most likely turned down other jobs to be here. Plus, she'd been looking forward to continuing to get to know him more.

Her gaze shifted, and she watched him preparing the soup. He was so handsome with his broad shoulders as he chopped some scallions. As adolescents, she'd never pictured him as the type to know his way around the kitchen.

Funny how her assumptions could be so wrong.

Thank goodness, people's assumptions about her had been wrong also. She hadn't turned out to be the messed-up woman people had whispered about.

Anyone would be scarred after the trauma she'd endured.

Can a person even recover from that?

She'll be messed up for life.

People didn't think Lindsey had heard them. But she had. She'd worked hard not to let those words embed themselves in her heart and be projected onto her future.

A few minutes later, Benjamin set a bowl of soup in front of her. He lowered himself across the table from her, and they prayed together.

Then he stated, "Now, how about if we talk about some suspects?"

CHAPTER THIRTY-TWO

"I THINK we should just lay it all out and see if we can figure out what's going on here," Benjamin said as he stared at Lindsey across the table.

She took a slow sip of her soup as if buying a moment with her thoughts. Finally, she nodded. "Okay. That's a good idea. You go first."

He took a spoonful of his own soup before grabbing an old notebook and a pen so he could jot down his ideas. He had a lot of them, but he wanted Lindsey's feedback.

"The number one suspect on my list is Sheriff Ross," he started.

"But he has an alibi for the night I went missing. He was at his uncle's funeral."

Benjamin frowned at the reminder. "I know. But there's still something about that guy I don't trust."

"I agree. There's something about him I don't trust either. But if he wasn't in town on the night my abduction happened, I don't see how he could be guilty."

He let out a long breath, his thoughts heavy and burdened. "So, we're going to assume that whoever is behind the incidents happening since we've arrived is the same person who abducted you as a child."

Lindsey circled her spoon in the soup, her eyes drifting with thought. "That's the only thing that makes sense to me. Unless you have other ideas."

"I suppose it would only be wise to explore other options, just in case. Somebody could simply want you out of here so they could have this place themselves."

"But the place has been abandoned for more than a decade," Lindsey glanced around the kitchen, which still needed a major overhaul. "If somebody wanted this place to themselves, it seems like they would have had ample opportunity."

"Maybe somebody was afraid we would find that trunk." Benjamin pointed to Lindsey with his spoon.

"But now that the trunk has been found, do they still have a reason to drive us away?"

They both sat there silently with their thoughts.

Maybe they were thinking too hard and needed a subject change for the moment. He took a long sip of his water and glanced at his paper once more.

"Let's see if there are any other suspects we can talk about," Benjamin finally said. "What about Fred from the hardware store?"

"Why would Fred have anything to do with this?" A wrinkle formed between Lindsey's eyes.

Benjamin shrugged and tried to choose his words carefully. "I don't know that he does, but he *is* associated with Daniel. Daniel's name was on a list of contractors Fred handed me the first time I went into the hardware store. Is that a coincidence?"

"I don't think we can assume anything is a coincidence at this point. But Fred was friends with my parents. He seems like a simple guy."

"But he was in town at the time you went missing," Benjamin said. "And if we're assuming that the person who abducted you wasn't a stranger but someone you knew . . . then he could fit the bill."

Lindsey let out a long breath. "You're probably right. I need to be open-minded here. But I just don't see him as being capable of this. Is there anyone else?"

Benjamin jotted down another name. "Irma."

Lindsey ran a hand over her face, appearing as if this conversation could be stressing her out. "I have a hard time thinking that someone like Irma could be behind this. She's too frail to knock someone upside the head and kill them, don't you think?"

She had a point. "Maybe. But Irma *has* been able to trudge over to the inn several times now. Part of the fence is falling down in the woods, so that's obviously how she's getting here. Plus, she said some weird things to you when she broke in."

Lindsey visibly shivered. "Tell me about it. She said, 'It's terrible what happened. I tried to stop them. I was going to come back for you, Lindsey. But they wouldn't let me.'"

His stomach churned at the implications of her statements. "If there is any hint of truth in Irma's words, then she knows what happened to you and she tried to stop your abduction from occurring."

"Why wouldn't she tell the police if that was the case?" Lindsey's voice almost sounded fragile.

Benjamin reminded himself to proceed with caution. "I can't tell you that. But she must have had a reason."

Lindsey let out a long breath and ran a hand over her face again, clearly feeling the tension of the situation. "What about Maple's mom?"

"As far as we know, Maple's mom isn't in town right now. That would make it a little bit hard for her to be behind this."

She finished her last sip of soup and pushed the bowl away. "You're right. But we need to keep her in mind when we're trying to put these pieces together."

"Agreed. Two other things we need to figure out are how Johnny the computer guy might have been involved and what connection Daniel has."

His statement hung in the air, and neither of them said anything. But Benjamin was definitely thinking and processing everything they'd just discussed.

THEY CERTAINLY HAD a lot to think about. Everything that had happened and all the possibilities of who was behind each incident felt almost overwhelming.

But there were a few more items Lindsey wanted to bring up.

As she sorted her thoughts, she stood and grabbed some of the muffins Irma had brought over. She set them on the table so they could munch on something sweet for dessert.

As she sat back down, she picked one up and set it on a napkin. She broke a piece off and popped it into her mouth. "I think we would be wise to run through everything that's happened as well."

"I'll take more notes." Benjamin held up his pen.

Lindsey smiled. She'd always thought as Benjamin of being more of a jock and not very studious. She liked this new side of him.

"When we first got here, there was an intruder in the house who pushed you out of the way. Based on everything you told me, it sounds like this person was a man. Is that correct?"

He nodded. "I think I would have noticed if it was a woman. This person had broad shoulders and heavy footsteps."

"Good point." Lindsey nodded. "Then we had the brick with a message thrown through the window and the electricity being cut. Both of those things make it clear somebody wanted us to leave."

"Right," Benjamin said.

"I don't think I ever mentioned this to you, but I also got a message on my phone," Lindsey started.

"Someone told me they knew what I did back in Staunton."

"What?" Benjamin frowned. "Another attempt to get rid of you."

Lindsey nodded again, not wanting to dwell on that too long—especially since she'd already told Benjamin the truth. That secret no longer had any power over her.

"And, finally, we can't forget that I found that message on the closet wall. *I didn't mean to do it. Please, forgive me. I beg you. Please!* I believe that handwriting is my mother's."

"Your parents *have* to have some type of tie into what happened here."

Lindsey fought a frown. "You're right. They do. But they're not here anymore so I can't ask them what that might be."

Benjamin let out a long breath before resting his elbows on the table. "Of course. Whatever's going on definitely ties back with your abduction and those two weeks you were missing. Maybe someone is afraid that you're going to remember. And maybe if you remember, you'll ruin this person's life. Because it's like Howie said—if the real culprit is still out there—and I believe he is— then this guy has gotten away with his crime for a long time. I'm sure he doesn't want his freedom taken away now."

Lindsey let out a long breath, her thoughts still racing inside her head. He had a good point. But she still thought there were some areas they could examine.

"Benjamin, I was trying to remember exactly why people thought your father was guilty. I know this is probably a hard subject. Do you remember much about that?" She studied him, hoping the question didn't cause him too much pain.

Benjamin stared off into the distance before shaking his head. "Mostly because your bracelet was found in his truck. When I got back to the room that night, he was gone. I didn't see him again until the next morning."

Lindsey's gaze latched onto his. "What exactly was his excuse?"

"He said that someone called him and said their car was broken down and asked him to help."

"Back then, cell phones weren't as easy to trace as they are now."

"Exactly." Benjamin nodded slowly.

Lindsey closed her eyes as images began playing in her mind like a movie reel. "So, someone most likely called him and got him to leave the inn in order to set him up. But I'm surprised we didn't hear him leave. Wasn't he in bed when you snuck out of the room?"

"I assumed he was in the room sleeping when I snuck out, but I suppose there's a chance that he was never there at all. I didn't check before I left the room."

"We may never know the answer. The fact that he died while he was in jail meant that anything he knew went to the grave with him."

"Unfortunately, that's correct."

Lindsey opened her mouth about to say more. But before she could, she heard the front door open, and someone called her name.

Her breath caught.

She recognized the voice.

Irma was back.

CHAPTER THIRTY-THREE

"IRMA, I didn't expect to see you back here." Lindsey paused after meeting the woman at the door. "Are you doing okay?"

Irma waved her hand in the air. "I'm so sorry about my spell last night. I don't remember most of it. But the doctor has me on all these crazy new medications, and they make me feel like I'm losing my mind. I'm going to ask him if we can change some."

"A visit to your doctor definitely sounds like a good idea." Benjamin appeared behind them. "I'm surprised you were able to come back home."

"They want me to stay with my niece. And she's a lovely woman. But I don't want to stay with Angela. I like living on my own."

"I guess you heard about the excitement here today?" Lindsey studied the woman's face for any sign that she knew more than she was letting on.

Irma frowned, the action capturing her entire face. Every wrinkle seemed to form a frown also. "I did. It's such a shame. Daniel was a nice guy."

"So you knew him?" Benjamin placed his hands on his hips.

"Oh, *of course*, I knew him. He was hardheaded and liked to get into trouble. But he was still a good boy."

More tragedy, Lindsey mused. When would it end?

She knew the answer.

It wouldn't end until the person responsible for these crimes was behind bars.

Lindsey turned back to Irma. "Can I ask you a question?"

"Of course."

"Why don't you sit down for a minute." Lindsey pointed to the couch in the formal living room. "Can I get you some food? Something to drink?"

"Oh no, I'm fine." She waved a freckled hand in the air. "But I *will* sit down for a minute."

Lindsey helped her over to the couch and waited until she was seated before starting. "Do you remember what you said last night when you were in my room?"

Irma frowned again. "I'm sorry. I don't."

"You said that it was terrible what happened to me and that you tried to stop them, that you were going to come back for me, but someone wouldn't let you."

Irma stared back with a blank expression before frowning. "I wish I knew what that meant, but I don't. I must have been watching one of those mystery shows before I went to bed. They make me have the strangest dreams."

Lindsey frowned, even though she'd figured that's what Irma would say. The woman had clearly been out of it. What she needed to figure out was if there was any truth in those puzzling comments. "One more question. Do you remember what my parents were like after I was abducted?"

Surprise flashed in Irma's gaze. "They were devastated, of course. Absolutely beside themselves."

"What did they do? Did they stay at the inn and continue on with business as usual? Did they go out looking for me? What exactly were they like?"

Irma shrugged and frowned. "They didn't go out looking for you. They seemed so burdened with grief that they let it paralyze them. It was really hard to watch. I know they were willing to do anything in order to get you back, just like any good parent would."

Lindsey nodded, hating how she felt unconvinced. "Thank you. I wasn't sure. They never seemed the same, even after I came back home."

"I would definitely say that the ordeal changed them and shook them to their core. I couldn't believe it when they actually left Hidden Shores."

Lindsey frowned. "Me neither. Life was definitely never the same after that."

"I can only imagine what you went through. I'm so sorry, my dear." Irma reached forward and patted her hand.

Lindsey inhaled a deep breath, trying to pull herself together. She hadn't anticipated this conversation would take such an emotional toll on her. But it had.

Talking about her parents had never been easy. But it had been necessary.

"So how about that supper club party we're supposed to have tomorrow night?" Lindsey had decided a subject change was in order. "Are you still up for it?"

Beside her, Benjamin's breath caught. Her words

had thrown him off guard. No doubt, he assumed she would cancel, considering everything that had happened—especially finding the dead body.

"You'd still like to have it?" Hope rose in Irma's voice.

"As a matter of fact, I would." Determination steeled Lindsey's voice before she added, "For old time's sake."

———

WHEN IRMA LEFT several minutes later, Benjamin turned to Lindsey. He'd kept his thoughts silent until they had a moment alone. But now he desperately wanted to know what she was thinking.

"I thought for sure you would want to cancel that supper club party," he started.

Lindsey shrugged. "Initially, I did. But then I realized it might be the best opportunity to find answers."

Realization rushed through him. "Because all our main suspects are going to be present?"

"Exactly. This might be our best chance to find out some answers. We'll have everybody here under one roof."

Benjamin nodded. On one hand, he liked the

way Lindsey was thinking. But, on the other hand, she could be putting herself in danger. He didn't like the thought of that. There'd already been more than enough danger to go around.

Plus, he just had a lot on his mind right now. Part of him wanted to whisk Lindsey away from this place and all the danger surrounding it. But would she be safe even if she wasn't here?

He didn't know the answer to that question.

Every time he'd started to tell her his secret, he'd been interrupted—almost like it wasn't meant to be.

Except it was.

Just then, his phone rang. He was about to dismiss the call when he glanced at the screen.

His breath caught when he saw Dawson's number there.

He glanced at Lindsey and nodded behind him. "I need to take this call."

"Of course."

Benjamin rushed down the hallway and put the phone to his ear before he missed the call. But he didn't speak until he went into his room and closed the door—just to be safe. "I've been trying to get up with you."

"I like to do things on my timetable." Dawson's cocky voice almost sounded amused.

Benjamin paced to the window, fighting to remain in control of his emotions. "I want out. And you need to leave Natalie alone."

"If only it were that easy." He almost sounded taunting now.

More anger surged through Benjamin. "It *is* that easy. Just let me out and leave us alone."

"I want something from you."

Something else? Was this guy for real? "Look, I found the trunk. There was a skeleton inside. He was identified as Johnny Flora. I did what you asked. Now I need you to hold up to your end of the bargain."

Dawson laughed, the sound deep and rumbling and entirely too amused. "It's not going to happen like that. I need more from you. I need you to find out what Lindsey remembers about the time she was abducted."

Benjamin squeezed the skin between his eyes, feeling a headache coming on. "She doesn't remember anything. You already know that."

"Just think about your cousin."

As Natalie's image flashed through his mind, his throat tightened. People should never be used as pawns.

But that was exactly the game Dawson—or

whatever his real name was—played. "Natalie needs heart surgery."

"I know. You told me already."

"I've got to get the money to help her." Desperation tinged his voice.

"I'm trying to help *you* help *her*."

Anger burned inside Benjamin. He hated being backed into a corner. But this man had left him with very few options.

Benjamin had to think of a way to get out of this situation.

But right now, a happy ending felt impossible.

CHAPTER THIRTY-FOUR

LINDSEY STARTED to sweep the floor when she saw that Benjamin's pocketknife had fallen out of his pocket. It must have happened when he'd grabbed his phone.

She scooped it up and headed down the hall. She didn't want to interrupt his phone call. But maybe she could slip the knife back to him and then let him finish his conversation.

She reached his bedroom door and started to knock when his voice drifted from the other side.

"Natalie needs heart surgery."

Her heart pounded. She knew she shouldn't eavesdrop. She hadn't intended to. It was just that the conversation could be heard from the other side of the door . . .

"I've got to get the money to help her."

Lindsey's breath caught. Suddenly, she knew exactly what Benjamin's secret was. The one he'd tried to tell her several times. The one that caused his gaze to look battle weary.

His cousin was sick.

Benjamin had taken this job to try to earn extra money for her.

She let out a breath, almost wanting to laugh. At times, she'd built it up in her mind to be something much more serious. Of course, someone having heart surgery *was* very serious. But, still, Lindsey had worried that there was more to Benjamin's story than that. More to *Benjamin* than that.

Relief trickled through her now that she knew she was wrong.

She slipped the pocketknife into her pocket and hurried down the hallway before Benjamin caught her. But, soon, the two of them would need to have a talk.

Maybe Lindsey could relieve some of his worries.

It was one small thing she could do for someone who'd helped her out so much.

BENJAMIN TRIED to pull himself together as he stepped from his room.

His thoughts continued to race.

The only way he was going to get out of the situation with Dawson was to figure out exactly who the man really was—and to figure out what happened to Lindsey during those two weeks she'd been abducted.

As much as he thought having the supper club party at the inn tomorrow night was a bad idea, maybe it would be a good opportunity to glean some information.

One of his first priorities was figuring out what Lindsey's parents had been hiding. If her mom had really written those words on the wall of the closet, then she was clearly dealing with some heavy things.

Plus, Benjamin needed to figure out why Daniel had been murdered at the inn.

And he wanted to look into Johnny Flora's background more.

After he said good night to Lindsey tonight, he was going to look online and do some research.

He glanced at his watch. It was almost time to turn in for the evening. The sun had set, and darkness stared at him from the outside.

He paused in front of Lindsey who stood in the living room where he'd left her, looking over everything as if she were imagining the supper club party here the next evening.

She glanced back and offered a soft smile.

"Are you sure you're ready for this party?" he asked.

Her gaze swept around the room again before she nodded. "I am. I mean, this place is nowhere close to being done. But at least I finished painting the foyer and the dining room. Tomorrow, I can mop the floors and make sure everything's dusted. Everyone is going to bring food to share so I don't have to worry too much about preparing the meal."

"It should be interesting, that's for sure."

Lindsey glanced at him before reaching into her pocket and pulling something out. A strange look lingered in her gaze—one he couldn't read.

"I found this and thought you might want it," she said.

He glanced at the knife. "Thanks. I didn't realize I had lost it."

"You must have dropped it when you pulled out your phone."

"Thanks." He gripped it for a moment before sliding it back into his pocket.

But as Lindsey stared at him, he continued to sense she had something else on her mind, something else she wanted to say.

"What?" He gave her a side-glance, trying to interpret her expression. Whatever she had to say, it put him on edge. He tried to downplay the reaction, but he wasn't sure he was succeeding.

"I know that you've been trying to tell me something." She stared at him with wide eyes brimming with emotions.

His lungs tightened until he felt he couldn't breathe. "I have."

"I just wanted you to know that I know what your secret is, and it's okay. I understand."

His heart raced faster as his thoughts scrambled to stay ahead of this conversation. "How do you know?"

How in the world had Lindsey found out? And why didn't she look more upset? She almost looked . . . compassionate.

She shrugged, still not seeming overly concerned. "I know Natalie needs surgery, and I'm sorry. It makes sense now why you took this job. You're trying to save up money so you can help with expenses."

It took Benjamin a moment to realize that the job

Lindsey referred to was his job as a handyman and not his job as a private investigator. But then his mind rewound their conversation even more. Lindsey had mentioned Natalie.

"You . . . you remember Natalie?"

"I do. She was just a toddler when she came here to visit. You had another cousin with you then too."

Benjamin nodded, this whole conversation feeling surreal. "That's right. I can't believe you remember that. We were—they were—only here for a couple of days as they passed through on their way to New York."

"I remember I was busy that weekend. I had a project I was working on for school, and my mom and dad made me stay in my room working on it for most of the time. But I remember meeting Natalie and how cute she was. I'm sorry to hear she's having medical issues."

Benjamin's throat burned. "She has some heart problems, and she needs surgery. Insurance won't cover the procedure she needs to have done because it's still considered experimental."

Lindsey tilted her head, compassion welling in her gaze. "I'm sorry to hear that, Benjamin. I can only imagine how hard that is. I remember that you and all your cousins were close. What was your other cousin's name who came that weekend?"

He wasn't sure he was going to be able to get the word out. "Finn."

Lindsey snapped her fingers. "That's right. Finn. I remember thinking he was so handsome—in a more studious, serious way than you. He used to give Natalie a ride on his shoulders, which I thought was the sweetest thing."

"People always say we look alike." He hoped she didn't hear the strain in his voice.

She scrutinized his face for a moment. "Actually, you do. He was a couple years older than you, so he seemed different. Older. More mysterious."

Heat continued to spread across his skin. "Yeah, Finn is a good guy. Although he's made a few decisions in his life that he regrets."

"Haven't we all?" Lindsey frowned as if bad memories battered her. "Anyway, I just wanted to let you know that you don't have to worry anymore. It's none of my business why you wanted to take this job. But it makes total sense now. I'm sorry you felt like you couldn't tell me. I imagine that you didn't want me to feel obligated to hire you so that's why you kept quiet."

Benjamin's heart twisted in his chest as he tried to figure out what to say.

Before he could say anything, Lindsey rose on her tiptoes and pressed a kiss on his cheek. "It's been a long day, so I'm going to head to bed. But I'll see you in the morning."

He nodded, although he felt numb. "I'll see you in the morning."

CHAPTER THIRTY-FIVE

BENJAMIN HADN'T GOT much sleep last night as his thoughts continued a running commentary in his mind.

He never expected Lindsey to remember meeting him all those years ago. Their interactions had been so brief. Yet she'd left a mark in his mind. She'd been bright and curious. But that light had been dimmed in the shadow of her parents' stern disciplinary style and high expectations.

For a moment, despite everything that had happened, he'd seen a glimpse of happiness in her last night.

Happiness that would be short-lived when she found out he'd been lying to her.

He had dug himself into this hole, and now he didn't know how he was going to get out of it.

Although the sun had yet to come up, he dragged himself out of bed. If he was awake, he might as well keep his thoughts occupied by doing something useful—something like an internet search as he attempted to find answers.

Johnny—whose body had been discovered in the trunk—didn't have much of an online footprint. Most mentions of the man simply stated he'd owned a computer shop in town.

It almost seemed strange that someone who'd owned a computer shop didn't have more of a presence on the web. Then again, Johnny had been dead for fifteen years now. Benjamin didn't think that people were as obsessed with social media back then.

As he'd been searching, Benjamin had noticed that a newspaper in the Hampton Roads area of Virginia had picked up the story of the body in the trunk. Benjamin wondered if the discovery would continue to gain attention or if it would simply disappear.

Only time would tell at this point.

Benjamin had also tried to look into the dead

man they'd found outside the inn yesterday. Daniel Markson *did* have an online presence.

Most of his pictures showed him with his friends hanging out by their cars with a beer in hand and flipping the peace sign to the camera. He seemed like a good old boy who was intent on having a good time. But Benjamin hadn't found anything that led him to any answers about the mysterious incidents surrounding the inn.

LATER THAT MORNING, Benjamin said hello to Lindsey and then he feigned an excuse about going into town to pick up a few more supplies. It wasn't a total lie. There *were* some things he needed to get. Meanwhile, Howie continued to work on the wiring.

The first place Benjamin went was to the hardware store. Just as he'd hoped, Fred was behind the counter.

The man's eyes lit with recognition when he saw Benjamin. "What brings you by again?"

Benjamin paused in front of him. "I need to pick up a few things. But I was also hoping to ask you a few questions."

Caution clouded his gaze. "About what?"

"About Daniel."

The caution in the man's gaze turned into grief, and he lowered his head. "I heard he died. I still can't believe it. No one here in town can believe it."

"Could you tell me anything about him?" Benjamin leaned into the counter, trying to look casual.

Fred let out a long breath and glanced out the window. "He was one of our local boys. Pretty good kid, although he didn't like to work too much. He preferred to party with his friends. He did like to fix up cars, which is one of the reasons I liked him as much as I did."

"Do you have any idea what he might have been doing out at the inn?"

"Your guess is as good as mine," Fred said. "But he came in at the beginning of the week asking if I'd heard about anybody who needed some work. That must mean he was running out of money. That's his cycle. Make money and then spend it having a good time and then repeat the process over again."

"Did you happen to mention the inn to him?"

Fred let out a hesitant nod. "Unfortunately, I did. I knew you guys were doing work there and said that you might need a hand. I didn't tell him anything for sure. But I have to wonder if he headed out there to see if you guys wanted to hire him for anything." Fred's voice caught. "It's the only reason I know that he would have gone."

"Lindsey called him to see if he wanted a job before she came into town."

"Like I said, he was probably living off the fruits of his labor—until they ran out. Then he got desperate for money."

"I understand. Thank you for that information." Benjamin took a step back.

With that, Benjamin went to grab the supplies he needed.

At least he had a reason now why Daniel might have been at the inn.

The question was, what had happened once Daniel arrived that had made someone want to kill him?

LINDSEY HAD SPENT most of the morning getting a few rooms at the inn back in order.

She had to admit that it felt good to see some progress. She polished the wood on the banisters and stairway. She dusted everything else and opened the windows to continue airing the place out. She still wanted to update some of the furnishings, but what they had would do for now.

If these people wanted to step back in time, tonight would be their opportunity.

Once she finished getting the foyer, living area, and dining room ready, she paced into the kitchen. For the supper club visits she'd observed as a child, her mother had always made her specialty, crab bisque.

Lindsey had most of the ingredients on hand right now to make it. She'd texted Benjamin and asked him to pick up some crabmeat from the market while he was out.

She hoped her plan paid off. She hoped having everyone here for this reunion might provide some answers.

Because she was tired of living in fear.

She remembered how Benjamin had told her that she needed to remember so she could move on and so healing could truly begin.

She needed to move on, and perhaps she'd never truly done that.

Lindsey had done her best. She'd put in an effort.

But now she needed closure.

As she waited for the soup to boil, she reviewed

the guest list for this evening. Irma. Sheriff Ross. Fred. Mayor Sorento. Mrs. Whitley.

Did one of them have the answer Lindsey needed?

Even more, were one of her guests responsible in some way for her abduction?

That's what she intended to find out.

For her parents' sake.

Even though they were dead, they deserved some kind of closure. This inn with all its history needed a second chance. And Lindsey desperately wanted to redeem herself after her fiasco back in Staunton.

She prayed she wasn't going through all this trouble for nothing.

At the thought, she pressed her eyelids together even harder.

Please, God. This needs to end. For good. Because this place might not have real ghosts haunting it. But it could certainly use a revival.

But, first, the darkness needed to be chased out.

CHAPTER THIRTY-SIX

AS BENJAMIN TURNED onto the lane leading to the inn, his phone buzzed. He pressed on the brakes and pulled the car to the side of the road.

Was that Dawson again? Did he have some other demand?

Benjamin quickly glanced at his phone. But the number he saw didn't belong to Dawson.

He didn't recognize it.

He quickly glanced at the text message.

As he read the words there, his gut squeezed with apprehension.

I KNOW **who you really are, Finn Washburn.**

. . .

HIS HEART POUNDED HARDER.

Who had discovered his secret? How was that even possible? He'd brought Benjamin's car here and one of his cousin's old driver's licenses.

The real Benjamin was currently in Puerto Rico. He'd asked Finn to take care of things while he was gone.

Finn never imagined that it would lead to this, however.

But now somebody knew Finn's real identity.

Clearly, Dawson already knew. He'd known when he hired Finn. He wanted to capitalize on the fact that Finn was both a PI and that he was Benjamin's cousin so therefore he knew most of the details of Benjamin's life.

But if this person told Lindsey his real identity before he could . . . then this would only end in disaster.

He sighed again and thought about this predicament he'd gotten himself into.

How was he going to find a way to get himself out of it?

First—he needed to keep thinking of himself as Benjamin.

At least until he told Lindsey the truth.

THE REST of the afternoon flew by. Lindsey didn't realize how much she thrived on deadlines. But knowing that people were coming tonight had put her into a higher gear.

She had cleaned and cooked then went to get ready herself. After slipping on a black dress and fixing her hair, she wandered over to an old record player her parents had kept in the living room. She found some music from the fifties and began playing it to set the mood a little bit more.

Jazzy, soulful music filled the room. This genre had always been her parents' favorite.

Lindsey heard someone whistle behind her, and she turned.

Benjamin stood there wearing black slacks and a white button-up shirt. "Don't you clean up nice?"

She smoothed the edges of her dress and smiled. "Thanks. I honestly didn't think I was going to have a chance to wear this when I packed it to come here. Clearly, I packed it anyway."

"You look fantastic." He reached for her hand and twirled her, his eyes still soaking in her every curve.

She didn't let go of his hand as she paused in

front of him. "I can't believe we're doing this. I hope it all works out."

"Me too." His voice grew serious. "I hope this doesn't start more trouble."

She swallowed hard at the thought. No, she needed to stay positive. "We just have to keep a cool head. Don't press too many buttons. Be wise with our words."

"Sounds like a good plan to me." Benjamin glanced at his watch. "Only ten more minutes until your guests are supposed to show up."

Just as he said the words, tires sounded on the gravel outside.

If Lindsey had to guess, it was the sheriff. From what she remembered the man was always early.

She glanced up at Benjamin and let out a long breath. "Here goes nothing."

CHAPTER THIRTY-SEVEN

BENJAMIN KEPT his eye on everyone at the party. He tried to be social yet aloof at the same time. Instead of remaining seated at the table, he stayed busy refilling drinks and being the runner between the dining room and the kitchen.

Did someone in this room know his real identity? If he or she did, what did they plan on doing with that information? His gut churned at the thought.

Everyone was seated at the table now. Sheriff Ross and his wife, Linda. Irma had arrived with Angela. Fred and his wife, Sue, were sitting beside each other. Mayor Sorento was also here as well as Mrs. Whitley.

It was quite the crew, and Benjamin could tell

that they all had history with each other. Not necessarily a good history. Not based on the furtive glances they continued to give each other.

Were each of them suspicious of the other also?

That would be his guess.

As he stood near the kitchen door, he glanced at Lindsey as she sat at one end of the table. She looked a little ill at ease, but probably no one else here could tell but him. He thought he'd learned to read her pretty well in the time since they'd been getting to know each other.

This had to be nerve-racking for everyone here. A killer could potentially be in this room right now. And they all knew it.

"It's hard to believe all the tragedy that has happened at this place," Mrs. Whitley began, her voice deep and demanding as she held a goblet of water. "Every time I look at that oak tree outside, I imagine the justice that was served here on this property. Things like that don't happen without leaving a mark on the land."

Lindsey looked a little paler. "What do you mean?"

"I just mean that with acts of violence come repercussions. It's ominous, to say the least."

"To say the least." Lindsey's voice sounded strained as she repeated the words.

"And now it appears that the tragedy continues," Mayor Sorento added. "It just seems unreal, doesn't it? Maybe opening up these walls has unleashed some evil."

A round of nervous chuckles went around the table.

"Now, you certainly don't believe in ghosts, do you?" Lindsey stared at him.

"I didn't until I came to this place." The mayor glanced between Lindsey and Benjamin. "I have to say I admire your bravery in coming back here after what happened."

Benjamin nodded slowly. "The real tragedy was the fact that my father died in jail before he could ever defend himself."

Mayor Sorento pressed his lips together.

Benjamin hadn't meant to go there, but he had. It needed to be said.

Benjamin's father had been wrongfully accused. His arrest had helped people sleep at night. But it offered a false sense of security because Lindsey's real abductor was still out there.

"I don't suppose you guys continued to look into

what happened to me after Mr. Newsom died?" Lindsey's gaze scanned everyone in the room.

"There was no reason to." Sheriff Ross cut his crab cake with his fork and stabbed the piece. "We had our bad guy."

"But what did you even think that his motive was?" Lindsey paused, knife in her hand. "That's never made sense to me."

"We were never sure," Sheriff Ross continued. "We can only assume he grabbed you, hid you in the woods, and that he was hoping to extort money from your parents."

"But my parents didn't have any money." Confusion lilted in her voice.

"People do bizarre things sometimes," Mayor Sorento said. "They get crazy ideas in their heads."

"All these years I've just sensed that my abductor is still out there. I still think so," Lindsey added quietly.

"That must be some kind of burden to carry," Fred said. "I don't envy you for it."

"Me neither." Lindsey frowned and glanced down at her half-eaten dinner.

Everyone murmured amongst themselves.

Benjamin stepped back toward his seat, wondering if it was time to change the subject. As he felt his cell phone buzz in his pocket, he had to wonder who'd sent him a message.

His guess?

Dawson Smith.

***

THE FOOD WAS DELICIOUS, and, in so many ways, this did seem like old times—not that Lindsey had ever been able to join the adults for dinner parties. No kids were allowed.

The events could only take place at certain times of the year when there were no guests here at the inn. But Lindsey had often snuck from her room and peeked around the corner to watch everyone talk and laugh.

These people didn't even seem like her parents' type of people. Especially not the mayor and Mrs. Whitley. They thought of themselves as too important. Her parents had never been pretentious like that.

When had her parents started changing?

Maybe around six months before Lindsey's abduction, if she remembered correctly. That's really when they had started to withdraw.

But why?

Somebody in this room probably knew. But finding that information and getting it from them would be an entirely different story.

"Did my parents get along with everyone?" Lindsey suddenly blurted.

Everyone turned silent as they glanced at her, a new awkwardness filling the room.

"Your parents?" Irma pressed her lips together as if the idea was outrageous. "Of course. They were our friends."

"But even friends don't get along sometimes," Lindsey continued. "Are you saying that there was only peace between everyone in this group and my mom and dad around the time I was abducted?"

More silence.

Maybe she shouldn't have asked. But she needed to know. She needed to know what was going on with her parents. They weren't here any longer for her to ask.

Mrs. Whitley turned to the mayor. "You had a disagreement with them about something around that time period, didn't you?"

The mayor's cheeks turned red. "Maybe. I hardly remember. It was so long ago, and I'm sure it wasn't important."

"Could it have been about operations here at the

inn?" Lindsey pushed. "Or was it something more personal?"

He shrugged a little too quickly. "Like I said, I don't remember. The inn was up on its permits and taxes, as far as I know. So, I'm unsure why we would argue."

Lindsey stared at him another moment. There was clearly something else the mayor knew, something he wasn't sharing.

The question was: what?

CHAPTER THIRTY-EIGHT

WHEN THE LAST guest had left, Benjamin turned to Lindsey in the foyer. The scent of Mrs. Whitley's pungent, expensive perfume still lingered in the air, as did the aroma of crab cakes.

"How do you think it went?" Benjamin asked.

She crossed her arms over her chest and shrugged. "I don't know. I don't know what I was expecting, but I guess I was hoping for a solid lead."

"Do you think Mrs. Whitley could have been behind your abduction?"

Lindsey shook her head. "She isn't the type to get dirty. She has all the money she needs. I can't imagine what her motivation might be."

"Good point. What about Mayor Sorento?"

"I suppose he's a possibility. I think he might

remember what the argument with my parents was about, but he isn't saying. But again, I'm not exactly sure what his motivation would be to abduct me either. Maybe I'm too naive. I'm not sure what to think about this whole evening."

Benjamin stepped closer and rubbed her arm. "I, for one, think you made a wonderful hostess."

A grateful smile crossed her lips and her eyes brightened. "Thank you for all your help, Benjamin. Now I guess I need to clean up."

He glanced at the kitchen where piles of dishes were stacked—and the old dishwasher didn't work. "Do you know what? Why don't you let me clean up?"

Surprise laced her gaze. "I couldn't possibly ask you to do that."

"You didn't ask. I volunteered. And I don't mind. You've been working hard all day today, and you could use some rest."

Lindsey ran her hand through her hair. "You really don't mind?"

"No, not at all. You go unwind, and I'll get these dishes. It's really no problem at all."

She reached forward and squeezed his hand. "Thank you, Benjamin. I can't tell you how much I appreciate this."

He wished it was that simple.

But the fact of the matter was that Dawson had texted him again and said that the two of them needed to meet at midnight at a location down the road from the inn. The text had ended with a demanding "or else."

LINDSEY WAS JUST DRIFTING off to sleep when she heard a sound.

She sat up straight in bed, a cold sweat covering her. She halfway expected to see Irma sitting beside her bed again looking like a ghostly form.

But it was silent in her room.

At least, that's what she thought.

Her heart hammered into her chest. What had made that sound? She'd been certain that she heard someone calling for help.

She waited.

But there was nothing. Maybe it had just been a dream.

Lindsey scooted back down in bed and pulled the covers up, but her eyes remained open.

She glanced at the time and saw it was almost midnight.

"Help!"

That's when she heard it again. For sure this time.

Somebody was calling for help.

Was that a man? Or a woman?

Lindsey couldn't tell.

Quickly, she got out of bed and threw some clothes on. She shoved her phone in her pocket and grabbed a flashlight she kept on her nightstand. After slipping her shoes on, she stepped into the hallway.

She nibbled on her lip for a moment and stared at Benjamin's bedroom door. Should she awaken him?

She knew without a doubt the answer should be yes.

But she also knew she didn't have time to waste —especially since she didn't know the details of what was going on out there. Because she felt certain that cry for help had come from outside her window.

Making a split-second decision, she rushed to his bedroom door and knocked. She only waited a couple of seconds before she twisted the door handle and stuck her head into the dark space.

"Benjamin?"

There was no response.

She pushed the door open farther, allowing some of the soft light in the hallway to spill into his room.

"Benjamin?"

When there was still no answer, Lindsey stepped closer to his bed.

But it was empty.

Maybe Benjamin had heard the cry for help also and had snuck out to see what was going on. It was the only explanation that made sense.

Wasting no more time, Lindsey ran through the inn and out the back door. She paused on the deck and glanced around.

The wind had picked up and made her hair swirl around her.

She waited to hear the voice again, to hear the cry for help.

A few minutes later, the eerie plea drifted through the air again, louder now that she was outside.

Someone clearly needed assistance. Desperation seemed to linger in the depths of this person's voice.

But where had it come from?

Lindsey thought she knew the answer, but she hoped she was wrong.

After swallowing so hard her throat hurt, she scrambled from the deck. When she reached the grassy area between the deck and the cliff, she paused once more.

Her gaze went to that gigantic oak tree standing on the property.

At once, she had a flashback of the person she'd seen hanging from it on the night she was abducted.

She squeezed her eyes shut.

Not now. She couldn't let her memories paralyze her. She couldn't allow herself to be swept back in time.

Right now, someone needed her help.

As she heard the cry again, she stepped closer to the rickety stairway leading down to the beach.

Lindsey paused at the top and shone her light below.

She could barely make out the waves on the bay.

As she glanced toward the other end of the beach, she thought she saw a figure there.

Irma? Was that Irma?

She was the only person who made any sense. No one else lived near this shoreline.

Maybe Lindsey should call 911.

But it might be too late by the time they got here.

The woman must have wandered from her

house again, maybe even had another one of her spells. Maybe Irma couldn't figure out how to get back. It could be as simple as that.

Sucking in a deep breath, Lindsey made the decision to try to descend the staircase. She'd be careful and watch every step. She hadn't yet ventured down this way to see how stable the structure was.

But she had no choice but to try right now and find out.

CHAPTER THIRTY-NINE

BENJAMIN STOOD on the side of the road, his flashlight in his pocket as he waited in the darkness.

The instructions he'd received made it clear he needed to walk to this location and not drive.

It hadn't been a long hike to get here. Just down to the end of the lane and north about a quarter mile.

But now he was stuck here on the roadside with the woods behind him as he waited.

He glanced at the time on his phone and saw it was already 12:15.

Where was Dawson? Why was he late?

Benjamin sent him a text and then waited to hear back.

Still nothing.

After fifteen more minutes had passed, he decided to call the man. But just as he expected, there was no answer.

Apprehension crept up his spine. Had Dawson wanted him out of the inn for some reason?

As soon as the thought slammed into Benjamin's mind, a new urgency gripped him.

What if that was it? What if this guy had wanted Benjamin out of the way so he could grab Lindsey?

How could Benjamin have been so stupid?

He took off in a sprint back toward the inn.

He needed to find Lindsey. See for himself that she was okay.

He made it back in record time. He rushed through the front door and down the hallway. If this was nothing and his instincts were wrong, then he'd happily face the consequences of waking Lindsey up.

He didn't bother to knock at her door.

Instead, he threw it open. "Lindsey?"

It only took a moment for Benjamin's eyes to adjust to the darkness and for him to see that Lindsey's bed was empty.

LINDSEY GRIPPED THE RAILING. With every step, she questioned her decision to go down to the beach.

So far, each of the stair treads had held.

It could have been her imagination, but part of her felt like this whole staircase swayed with the wind.

She swallowed, trying to get her anxiety to subside.

Just as she drew in a few deep breaths and exhaled, she heard the cry for help again. The voice sounded even more urgent this time.

Her apprehension climbed to greater heights.

Lindsey tried to pick up her pace, but fear stopped her from going too fast.

This cliff, at one time, had been eighty feet. She specifically remembered that number because her parents had repeated it multiple times. She hadn't been allowed to play near the edge of the cliff because there was an *eighty-foot drop*. The *eighty-foot drop* was enough to seriously kill or hurt somebody.

She would never forget them talking about that, grinding the reminder into her head.

She took a couple more steps downward.

On the third step, the wood beneath her squeaked. She tested her weight on it.

CHRISTY BARRITT

The plank bowed.

Still gripping the wooden handrail, she skipped that step and lowered her foot to the next. There were two landings between the top of the staircase and the beach. She'd almost reached the first one.

Her heartbeat pounded in her ears.

The best-case scenario was that she'd get to the bottom of the cliff, find Irma, and discover she was just having a spell, and then get the woman back to the inn where she could call Angela.

Lindsey prayed that would be what happened. Prayed that she wasn't missing something major right now.

Her heart continued to pulse in her ears, each beat seeming to warn her that this was a bad idea.

Finally, she reached the first landing.

She paused there and sucked in a deep breath.

She could do this. Not much farther, and her feet would reach the sand below.

She drew in another deep breath before starting down the next step.

But as the wind gusted again, she lost her balance and shifted toward the handrail.

As she did, she heard a crack.

Then air swept beneath her.

The railing fell to the ground below . . . taking Lindsey with it.

A scream escaped as she tumbled to the sandy shore below.

CHAPTER FORTY

AS SOON AS Benjamin heard the scream, his blood froze.

That was Lindsey. He was certain of it.

He darted through the inn and toward the back door.

Had Dawson grabbed her?

Some of his apprehension turned to anger. Benjamin should have never allowed himself to leave tonight. He should have known it was a scam.

What if Lindsey had gotten hurt as a result? Then who would be next? Natalie?

He tore open the door, rushed outside, and paused, scanning everything around him.

His gaze stopped at the tree, and he held his

breath. He halfway feared he might see Lindsey there, hanging from one of the branches.

He released his breath when he realized no one was there.

Where had Lindsey's voice come from?

At once, he knew.

He darted toward the cliff and peered down the staircase.

It was hard to know for sure, but it almost looked like someone was lying at the bottom of the dilapidated stairway . . . unmoving.

"Lindsey . . ." he murmured.

Wasting no more time, Benjamin took off down the stairs. He watched every step so there wouldn't be two casualties.

But he knew he didn't have any time to waste either.

Finally, he reached the bottom.

"Lindsey!" He rushed to her and knelt beside her, searching for any signs of life.

When her eyes blinked open, relief washed through him.

She was alive!

"Benjamin?" she muttered.

"Are you okay, Lindsey?" He leaned over her, peering into her eyes so he could see the truth.

She moaned and sat up. Rubbing her head, she glanced around, looking slightly dazed. "I think so. The sand broke my fall, I guess."

"What were you doing out here?"

"I heard someone calling for help down here. I thought it was Irma."

His spine tightened. He glanced up and down the shore to see if anyone else was out here.

He saw no one.

He only heard the waves gently lapping against the sand and the breeze blowing.

First, he would make sure that Lindsey was okay.

Then he'd check out whoever had lured her down here.

LINDSEY'S HIP was going to ache, but she didn't think she'd broken anything. She was lucky to walk away from the accident with only a few bruises, especially considering the distance she'd fallen.

The sand was surprisingly soft beneath her, otherwise she might not have been so fortunate.

Benjamin helped her to her feet.

"I tried to find you, but you were gone," Lindsey blurted.

"I got a text saying someone needed my help down the road." He shrugged. "I decided to find out what was going on . . ."

She gasped. "Just like your dad . . ."

He grimaced. "Yeah, just like my dad. Now, let's get you back inside before we have any more surprises."

He kept an arm around her as he started to lead her back to the staircase.

"Wait." She stopped him. She'd come this far, and she wasn't ready to leave yet. "What about the person I heard calling?"

Benjamin leveled his gaze with her. "There's no one here, Lindsey."

"But I know what I heard . . . and I saw someone." She didn't break her gaze, needing to let him know she was serious.

He opened his mouth but shut it again. Finally, he said, "I'm not saying you didn't. But there's no one here now."

"Can we just check, at least? Just so I can know for sure?" She was going to do this with or without him. With him was the best option, however.

He pressed his lips together like he didn't want to do that. But finally, he nodded. "Okay. Would you like to sit here while I look around?"

"No, I'm okay. I can go with you."

He pulled out his flashlight and swept the beam over the shore as they began walking down the dark beach.

"Irma?" Lindsey called.

But there was no answer.

"When was the last time you heard this person call for help?" Benjamin asked.

"Right before the railing broke and I fell."

She heard Benjamin's breath catch.

"What?" Lindsey turned toward him.

He didn't say anything, but she knew what he was thinking.

"You think this was all a setup, don't you?"

He shrugged. "Maybe."

"You think somebody wanted this to happen."

"Based on everything that's been going on, can you blame me?"

She shook her head, hating the apprehension that consumed her. "I guess not."

They reached the end of the sandy cove in front of the inn. Rocks formed a jetty between the properties—large rocks that would be nearly impossible to cross in the dark.

Irma was nowhere to be seen.

Lindsey frowned. She wished she could say that made her feel better. But that wasn't the truth.

Nothing about the situation felt good.

Benjamin kept an arm around her as he led her back to the stairway. "I'm going to help you get up the steps. Safely."

"Then we should probably call the sheriff?"

He stared at her a moment. "We can. But I think we both know that's not going to do any good."

She wanted to argue with him, but she couldn't.

Because she knew he was telling the truth.

CHAPTER FORTY-ONE

LINDSEY HAD HARDLY GOTTEN any sleep last night. When she'd finally climbed out of bed, her entire body ached. Just as she'd thought would happen.

The first thing she wanted to do this morning was to check on Irma. Even though she felt certain it probably wasn't Irma who'd called her outside last night, she needed to be sure.

As soon as she was dressed, she went into the kitchen to grab some coffee. Benjamin was already up, looking ready to work as he placed a mug in the sink.

His eyes warmed as soon as he saw her. "Good morning."

"Morning."

He grabbed a clean coffee mug, filled it, and then handed the warm drink to her. As he did, he leaned toward her and gently pressed a kiss on her forehead.

"You doing okay today?" he murmured.

"I guess. But I have to admit that I'm hurting all over right now."

"I bet you are. I'm just glad it wasn't any worse than it was. You could have been killed."

She shuddered. Was that what someone had planned? What someone had hoped would happen?

It seemed like a good possibility.

Lindsey took a few sips of her coffee, and she and Benjamin discussed the plans for today. Howie was coming in again to work on the wiring. She couldn't wait to have that project done.

Every time she thought about Howie coming, the labor cost began to add up in her mind. But the job couldn't be avoided. She hoped they didn't run into any more problems here, but she'd be naive to think they wouldn't.

When she finished her coffee, she turned to Benjamin, knowing that she needed to mention what she was going to do. "I want to pay Irma a visit. I need to know she's okay, that it wasn't her out there last night."

Benjamin stared at her a moment before nodding. "How about if I go with you? I'd feel better if I did."

She had figured he would say that so she nodded. "Okay."

Instead of driving, they walked across the property and through the woods. Lindsey had wanted to see the condition of the fence anyway. Apparently, it was in rough shape.

When they came across it, she saw it was ramshackle at best—just a chain-link barrier through the woods. At the front of the property, the fence was wrought iron to make a good impression.

Lindsey and Benjamin stepped over a section where the fence had collapsed and walked another two hundred feet or so through the woods before they reached the carriage house. It matched the inn with its wooden siding and old plantation-style shutters. But it nearly looked as rough as the inn did—and the inn had been abandoned.

Despite its rundown state, cheerful mums and geraniums decorated the front porch.

She glanced in the driveway and saw two cars there. She wondered if Angela was visiting her aunt.

She started toward the front door when she heard voices in the backyard.

But it wasn't two females talking. One of them was a male.

Her muscles stiffened as she walked across the grass toward the backyard. Was she imagining things or were both of those voices familiar?

Lindsey paused when she reached the other side of the house.

Irma sat on her patio, looking safe and healthy.

That was a relief.

But as Lindsey's gaze slid to the person Irma was talking to, she saw. . . "Colin?"

She felt herself reeling.

What was he doing here?

"COLIN?" Benjamin repeated, not bothering to hide his disbelief.

But Lindsey didn't seem to hear him. Instead, she stepped closer, her shoulders tight and her actions stiff.

The man talking to Irma was probably in his mid-to-late thirties. He was thin, with thick black hair and tired eyes. A former CEO with criminal tendencies?

Possibly.

The man jumped to his feet, his gaze on Lindsey. "I wasn't expecting to run into you yet."

"What are you doing here?" Lindsey's hands fisted at her sides as she stared at him.

"I came here to talk to you."

"Do you mean *threaten* me?"

The man's eyes narrowed. "I didn't have a chance to do that quite yet."

Benjamin stepped forward, not liking this guy already. "What does that mean?"

The man's arrogant gaze turned toward Benjamin. "Who is he?"

"That's none of your business," Lindsey said. "What I want to know is why you're following me."

Colin let out a quick breath of air. "Following you would be an overstatement. I came here just to express my displeasure at the way things ended between us. I never thought that you'd betray me like that and be a whistleblower."

"Then you never really knew me that well." Lindsey's voice sounded at just above a growl.

"You can say that again." His tone became almost mocking.

"And a phone call wouldn't have worked? You had to come all the way here?" Lindsey said.

Benjamin stepped back, letting Lindsey take

charge. If she needed him, Benjamin would step in. But she was handling herself just fine right now.

"At first, I wanted to ruin any chances you had at succeeding here," Colin admitted. "Then I figured that I didn't have to."

"Wait, you came here to ruin me, and now you're sitting here with Irma?"

"I actually got here yesterday, and I've been asking around town about you, trying to dig up some dirt."

"And?" Defensiveness edged Lindsey's voice.

"It seems like bad things keep happening around you—without my help. It's a win-win situation, if you ask me."

Anger flashed in Lindsey's gaze. "You had no right to come here."

Colin raised his hands and took a step back. "I had every right. Because of you I may be spending time in prison. I wanted to see your life ruined as well."

Benjamin bristled again, desperately wanting to step in. But he held himself back—for now.

"And now that you're here?" Lindsey asked.

Satisfaction glimmered in the man's gaze. "Now I've heard your story. I've heard about this haunted inn that you're trying to fix up. I've heard all about

your past and your abduction, things you never talked to me about."

"Maybe that's because part of me knew I couldn't trust you."

He shrugged as if unaffected. "I won't take any offense at that. But the fact of the matter is, I've got better things to do. I have people I need to see before I have to go back for my court date. I shouldn't have wasted this valuable time coming here to ruin you. You've done just fine with that on your own."

This guy was a first-class jerk. He had a lot of nerve coming here.

Colin glanced back at Irma. "Thank you for the coffee. But I'll be going now."

Benjamin watched as the man paced toward the front of the house. A moment later, a car engine started and tires turned on gravel as Colin pulled away.

Benjamin turned to Lindsey, anxious to hear what she'd say next.

⸻

A MILLION THOUGHTS raced through Lindsey's mind. She couldn't believe Colin had the nerve to show up here. Nor could she believe he was leaving this quickly.

Unless he really did think she was a lost cause.

Based on everything that had happened, that just might be the case.

"Are you okay?" Concern filled Benjamin's gaze.

Lindsey nodded and rubbed her arms, feeling chilled at the whole encounter. "I guess."

"Why don't we go inside for a minute?" Irma piped in. "I'll get you some water. You look like you need some."

Neither Benjamin nor Lindsey argued. Instead, they followed Irma into her kitchen. She grabbed two glasses, added some ice, and then poured water from the tap. She then handed the drinks to them and watched as they both took sips.

"I'm sorry I let him on my property," Irma started with a frown.

"It's okay," Lindsey said. "You didn't know."

"What brings you by?" Irma asked. "I assume you didn't know he was here, so you had to come for some other reason . . ."

Lindsey set her glass on the butcher-block countertop before turning to Irma. "I had a question for you. Were you out on the beach last night?"

"Last night? I know better than to head out there

at night." She let out a guffaw. "The walk down to the water is too dangerous. Why do you ask?"

Lindsey frowned. "I thought I heard you calling for help, and I went to check, but I didn't find you. I needed to know that you were okay."

"Oh, I'm just fine, dear. I didn't take my medicine last night, so I am as lucid as lightning on a clear night."

The woman sounded convincing.

If Lindsey's instincts were right, someone had purposefully lured her out to the beach last night, hoping Lindsey would be hurt.

Lindsey took another sip of her water as her thoughts raced.

"I want to apologize again." Irma frowned. "I'm sorry I talked to that man. He only arrived about ten minutes before you got here."

"It sounds like you told him stories about the inn," Lindsey clarified.

"I didn't realize that he was associated with you. He was just asking questions about the inn's history, and you know how much I love to talk about history. I thought maybe he was a reporter."

Lindsey nodded. Irma had made herself an unofficial town historian it seemed.

She took one last sip of her water before setting

it on the counter. She was about to tell Irma she needed to get back when a photo on the wall behind her caught Lindsey's eye.

She paced closer and stared at six people pictured, all in a line, with the Chesapeake Bay behind them.

Her parents were two of the people. Irma and her husband were also in the photo. But the other two . . . ?

"Who are they?" Lindsey pointed to a man and woman she didn't recognize.

"You don't remember? That's Ted and Janine. They were good friends of your parents."

"Oh, yeah. I do vaguely remember them. But . . . what happened to them?" She hadn't heard their names in years.

Irma's face squeezed with pain. "Probably six months before you were abducted, they were both killed in a hit-and-run. It was so tragic . . ."

"What?" This was the couple Sheriff Ross had mentioned to Lindsey after they'd found the trunk, when he'd been talking about how people around here remembered the bad things that happened because there were so few of them.

"It was just terrible," Irma continued. "Their car broke down, so they were walking on the side of the highway to get help. As they were, someone hit them and drove away, leaving them for dead. They were both killed on impact."

"Did they ever catch who was responsible?" Benjamin rested his hands on his hips in a casual manner as he waited for her answer.

But Lindsey knew he was anxious to hear more, and he was just pretending to be casual.

"The police never did find out who it was." Irma's gaze latched onto Lindsey's. "I've never seen anything that drew your mother to her prayer closet like their deaths."

Lindsey's breath caught at Irma's words. "Her prayer closet?"

"Why, yes. You didn't know about that?" Irma began to absently straighten a stack of napkins on the table.

Lindsey shifted. "No, I didn't. Can you tell me more?"

"It was in one of the spare bedrooms. Your mom read a book—I can't remember the name. After that, she designated a space to get away from everyone and pray. She used to tell me she spent a lot of time there, especially when she felt worried. She was so shaken by Ted and Janine's deaths that she said she wanted to disappear into that closet forever."

Something nagged at the back of Lindsey's mind, some type of realization that begged for her attention.

That's when it hit her.

She needed to talk to Benjamin. Now.

At once, she turned to him and forced a smile that she hoped looked pleasant. "We should probably get back. We have a lot to do."

The look he gave her made it clear he knew something else was going on here. But he didn't ask any questions. Not yet.

Instead, the two of them thanked Irma for the water and then started back to the inn.

Lindsey hoped she didn't sound crazy when she shared her theory with him.

But she thought she'd just found a missing puzzle piece.

CHAPTER FORTY-TWO

"WHAT ARE YOU THINKING?" Benjamin asked Lindsey as soon as they were away from Irma's house and heading back toward the woods.

Lindsey's gaze traveled back and forth with deep thought as they walked. "Six months before my abduction was when my parents started acting funny."

"Okay . . . do you think your parents had something to do with their friends' deaths?" His thoughts raced as he tried to figure out where she was going with this.

"I don't know. But what if my parents knew something about whoever was involved with that hit-and-run?"

"Why would you think that? Maybe they were just grieving the loss of their friends."

They stepped into the woods and began the trek back toward the inn.

"Just bear with me for a moment as I try to sort out my thoughts," Lindsey continued. "Maybe they're crazy and won't make any sense. But maybe that's not the case."

"Okay." Benjamin was anxious to hear what she was about to say.

"Remember that text I got warning me that someone knew my secret . . . that secret being what happened between me and Colin."

"Of course." His stomach clenched as he remembered the similar threat that he received. He hadn't told her about that yet, though.

"What if all of this is about secrets?"

"You're going to have to explain some more."

"Sheriff Ross . . . he had an affair, but he still became sheriff. Maple's mom . . . she stole money from her former employer and was run out of town. What if someone was able to find out everyone's secrets and that's where all of this pain and crime is centered?"

"I like where you're going with this, but how would someone find out everyone's secrets?"

She still stared straight ahead as if lost in her thoughts. "I don't know. Maybe it could be a minister. He's somebody that people share secrets with. Or a counselor."

"Do you even have counselors around here?"

She shrugged. "Not that I know of. We don't even have a psychologist that somebody might go to and share secrets with. So, who else do people share secrets with?"

"You got me there. I'm not really sure."

"Do I sound crazy?" She paused in the middle of the trees and turned to him.

"No, you don't sound crazy. You very well could be onto something. But what would someone hope to get from the secrets?"

"I have a feeling somebody was using them to persuade people so that person could get what they wanted. That's the only thing that makes sense to me."

"But who would do that?"

Her gaze locked with his. "That's the question that we need answered."

BACK AT THE INN, Benjamin couldn't stop thinking about Lindsey's theory. It made sense. There did seem to be a lot of secrets involved here.

Including a possible one about her parents.

Around the time of Ted and Janine being killed, Lindsey's mom had retreated into her prayer closet. A prayer closet where words had been written on the wall begging for forgiveness.

Lindsey's parents had been involved with that accident, hadn't they?

It was the only thing that made sense.

He knew that he needed to find Howie and get to work. Yet he told Lindsey that he needed to slip into his room for a minute to take care of some business. Instead, he grabbed his computer and tried to find whatever articles he could about the accident.

He found them, but there wasn't really any new information there. It was mostly what he already knew.

The truth of the matter was that someone was able to find out people's secrets and use their secrets as leverage.

Just as they were trying to do now.

So, things were starting to make more sense.

That person was most likely Dawson Smith—or whatever the man's real name was.

Could Sheriff Ross be a part of this? Fred? The mayor?

Or maybe it wasn't a man. Maybe it was Mrs. Whitley. The woman was frail, but she could have hired someone to do the dirty work for her.

Thoughts swirled in his head.

Finally, he closed his computer.

Enough was enough.

Secrets had cost lives. They caused trauma.

And Benjamin didn't want his name to be added to the list of troublemakers.

He was going to tell Lindsey the truth. Best-case scenario was that they could navigate that revelation together. Worst case was that Lindsey would never forgive him.

He didn't want to overthink this. He feared if he stayed in his room any longer, that's exactly what he would do. He would somehow talk himself out of sharing this news—and that was the last thing he wanted.

He started toward the door, praying he'd have the right words to say and that Lindsey might have compassion on him, despite the fact he didn't deserve it.

CHAPTER FORTY-THREE

MAPLE SURPRISED LINDSEY and showed up with a welcome gift.

Lindsey invited her inside, where they sat at the kitchen table with coffee and homemade banana nut bread—brought by Maple.

As the two of them chatted, the breeze blew through the open kitchen window. Dry autumn leaves danced across the deck outside, their scraping sound tightening Lindsey's nerves.

Normally, she'd enjoy the sound. But not right now. Not when she had so much on her mind.

At a break in the conversation, Lindsey licked her lips. She had something she wanted to ask Maple, and she hoped it didn't sound insensitive.

"Can I ask you a question?" Lindsey started.

"Of course." Maple took a sip of coffee.

"Did you happen to ask your mom any more questions about the money that she said she stole from her boss?"

Maple shrugged and shook her head. "I figured if my mom wanted me to know, she would've told me. I am not much for getting into other people's business. It keeps life simpler. Why are you asking?"

"It's just a theory I'm playing with about something that's going on here in this town."

"I see. I wish I could help you. I do know that there's been a part of me that's trying to keep my distance. Some people here don't seem to like outsiders. Maybe they feel threatened by them. I'm not sure. But either way, I don't like a lot of drama."

"I understand. And avoiding it can definitely be a good thing."

Lindsey jerked her head toward the doorway as she heard a footstep.

She halfway expected to see a killer standing there.

Instead, it was Benjamin.

Something close to disappointment filled his features as his gaze traveled from Lindsey to Maple.

He clearly hadn't expected Lindsey to have any visitors.

She quickly introduced them.

"Nice to meet you," Benjamin said. "It's nice that you brought treats. Banana nut bread is my favorite."

He reached over and broke a piece in half, quickly popping it in his mouth.

Panic raced through Lindsey. "Wait, Benjamin. You can't eat that!"

He only stared at her. "What are you talking about?"

"It has nuts in it," she reminded him. "You're deathly allergic."

He swallowed hard, looking ill-at-ease. "I grew out of it."

Lindsey stared at him another moment when the truth hit her.

There had been signs. Too many signs. Signs she'd wanted to ignore.

First, it was the fact Benjamin didn't remember how much he liked eclairs. Then he hadn't remembered sliding down the banister and busting out the window.

Now he was eating nuts as if it wasn't a big deal.

She rushed to her feet as outrage shot through her.

"You're not Benjamin at all, are you?" Her voice came out just above a whisper, but the accusation was undeniable.

His shoulders seemed to slump. "Lindsey . . . let me explain."

He didn't even bother to deny it.

Lindsey had let it happen again. She'd allowed herself to be charmed by someone to the extent that she hadn't seen the truth. How could she have been so dumb . . . again?

"Lindsey . . ." Benjamin started.

But before he could finish, Lindsey rushed toward the door. "Maple, you'll have to excuse me. But I need to go."

She fled to her room, needing a moment by herself.

BENJAMIN HAD TRIED to talk to Lindsey, but she only told him to go away. After attempting a conversation several times, he finally headed upstairs to help Howie. But his mind was never far from what had happened.

There was no one to blame for this mess except

himself. If he could go back and do everything over again, he would have never accepted this assignment.

But if he hadn't accepted his assignment, he would have never realized what an incredible person Lindsey was.

The conundrum made him feel like a battle was warring inside him. He only knew that he didn't want to lose Lindsey from his life.

But it appeared that it was too late.

Finally, at five p.m., Howie left for the day. Normally, Benjamin would have dinner.

But he had no appetite right now.

How could he have forgotten about Benjamin's— the real Benjamin's—nut allergy? He'd been so distracted with his thoughts about telling Lindsey the truth that he'd let his guard down.

He somehow had to figure out a way to make this right.

He cleaned up a little from their work. The electric wiring should take a few more days until it was done.

Would Benjamin even have a job here at that point? He didn't know.

Finally, he couldn't wait any longer. He needed to

try to talk to Lindsey again. What had she been doing in her room this whole afternoon?

A fresh round of worry washed through him.

Feeling bile rise in his stomach, he went to her room and knocked on the door again. "Can we just talk for a few minutes?"

To his surprise, the door opened. Lindsey stood there, her red-rimmed eyes scowling at him. A mixture of anger and sadness mingled in the depths of her gaze.

"I've got nothing to say to you," she started.

"Can you please let me explain?"

"You're not the person I thought you were," she murmured. "That's really all that matters right now."

Her words echoed in Benjamin's ears. They were almost word for word what Ashley had also said to him.

An ache formed in his heart, spreading across his chest.

He deserved the words. He couldn't deny that. But that didn't make the statement hurt any less.

"Benjamin is my cousin," he rushed.

Lindsey's hand was on the door as if she might slam it in his face, but she paused. "Wait . . . you're Finn?"

"Yes, Finn. Benjamin and Natalie are both my cousins. Benjamin came to live with my family after he left this area and his father died."

"Why are you here? Why did you lie to me?"

"It's a long story. But I'm actually a private investigator, and someone singled me out for this job, saying I'd be perfect for it but I needed to pretend to be my cousin."

Her lips parted with surprise. "Why would someone do that?"

"At first, this guy made it seem like it was because you were involved in some type of crime that you were trying to cover up. But the more I think about it, the more I think now that whoever abducted you is the person who hired me. I've been trying to get out of this job, but he is threatening Natalie."

Lindsey's eyes widened. "He threatened Natalie?"

"He sent her a postcard and signed my name to it. He sent me a picture of her at school. He has someone watching her. Waiting to snatch her if I don't follow through with this. If he finds out I told you, I don't know what he'll do. So, even though I don't deserve your forgiveness, I'm asking you—begging you—to let me have a little more time. I need to figure this out before Natalie is hurt."

As she stared at him for several moments, he had no idea what Lindsey was going to say.

Before she responded, a knock sounded at the front door.

Who was here now?

CHAPTER FORTY-FOUR

LINDSEY WELCOMED THE INTERRUPTION. She could use a breather before she responded to Benjamin's bombshell revelation—only, he wasn't Benjamin.

The man in front of her had lied to her. Come here under false pretenses. Had made her feel foolish.

Now he expected her to forgive him?

She wasn't sure that would be possible. But for the sake of Finn's cousin, Lindsey would delay making that decision until her emotions calmed down some.

She pushed by Finn and headed toward the door, ready to be away from him.

"Can we at least talk about this more later?" Finn

called behind her, his voice strained with emotion. "Please?"

"Maybe." Lindsey couldn't give a definitive answer right now. She was still too angry.

Instead, she threw open the door, her emotions still boiling.

Sheriff Ross stood there.

She should have figured. It seemed like her days weren't complete unless he visited. On the positive side, maybe he had some news for her.

"Do you have an update?" Lindsey noted that Finn had followed her and stood a few feet away, but still close enough to listen.

The sheriff quickly shook his head as if impatient. "I wish I had news to tell you. But there's none. We're still investigating."

She waited for him to explain why he was here, but he seemed to be waiting for Lindsey to say something. Awkwardness shifted between them.

Before either of them could speak, another car pulled in behind him.

Now who else was here?

Lindsey turned back to the sheriff. "Is there a reason that you stopped by then?"

He shrugged, almost as if annoyed. "I'm here because I got the invitation."

"The invitation?" she repeated.

Before he answered, Fred stepped from his truck and walked toward them.

What was going on here? Why had Fred come also?

If that wasn't strange enough, Irma climbed from the passenger seat of his truck. And before they even reached the door, a Lexus pulled in. Mrs. Whitley, no doubt.

"An invitation?" Lindsey turned back to the sheriff.

"I got a card in the mail today saying that I was supposed to be here at seven p.m. There was no return address on it, but I thought you'd sent it."

"I didn't send it." Lindsey glanced back at Finn. "Did you?"

He shook his head.

Several minutes later, the sheriff, Fred, Irma, Mrs. Whitley, and Mayor Sorento all gathered inside the old inn.

Unrest jostled inside Lindsey's stomach.

Someone had called this meeting. Someone had wanted them each here at the inn at this very time for some reason.

Lindsey had a feeling that whatever the reason was, it was nefarious.

"WOULD someone tell us what's going on here?" Finn turned to face everyone around him, not liking the situation. His gut—finely tuned from the battlefield—told him that something was majorly wrong and that danger lurked entirely too close.

Only moments earlier, his biggest concern had been earning back Lindsey's trust. That was still important to him. But preserving their lives had taken priority.

"That's what I would like to know also." Sheriff Ross put his hands on his hips as he scanned the gazes of everyone in the room. "Who sent those invitations?"

Everyone stared at each other, but no one admitted anything.

"It had to be someone in this room." Lindsey's tense voice cut into the silence. "What sense would it make otherwise?"

"I don't know." Mrs. Whitley pulled a paper fan from her purse, spread it open, and began waving it in front of her face. "But I don't like this. I don't intend on staying here. This is just wasting my time."

"Before you go, is there anything anyone needs to

say right now?" Finn knew that once people began to leave, it would be harder to get answers.

Everyone remained silent.

"I think we all know what this goes back to," Fred spoke up. "I don't know why no one wants to say it. The truth has been held as leverage over us for so many years that we don't know how to live without fear."

Finn's heart beat harder into his chest as he waited to hear what the rest of the group would say.

"What are you guys talking about?" Lindsey's wispy tone contained a hint of surprise, even though she'd surmised earlier that secrets had somehow drawn this group together.

"Do you mean you don't know yet?" Fred's gaze locked onto hers.

"Fred . . ." The mayor let out a warning growl.

Fred shook his head, his jaw hardening. "I just don't care anymore. I'm tired of living like this. I'm tired of someone else controlling everything I do. I want out. I want to end this."

"I don't know what you're talking about." Mrs. Whitley raised her chin and averted her gaze. She glanced at the door as if she wanted to flee.

"Stop denying it. We all know what's happening.

We're all in this, and we have been in this for fifteen years." Fred's tone turned from jovial to cutting.

Fifteen years? Finn could feel in his bones that some of the answers they desperately needed could soon be revealed.

"Would someone care to explain to us exactly what's going on?" Finn stared at everyone in the room.

Everyone remained silent, their gazes shifting as they cringed and scowled.

Finally, Irma stepped forward, worry wrinkling her gaze. "I agree with Fred. I'm tired of this. I'm tired of the secrets."

Finn's gaze continued to travel around the group as he examined everyone there. "How are you all connected with what's going on?"

Everyone in the room other than Finn and Lindsey glanced at each other. There was obviously a story here—one that people didn't want to share.

Sheriff Ross hesitated, muttering something beneath his breath before finally turning to answer. "I'm tired of being a prisoner to this also. About sixteen years ago, Johnny Flora came to us with an idea. He'd been working on a computer program, but he needed investors to help him pay for it. He insisted it could be very profitable."

"What kind of computer program?" Lindsey's eyes narrowed with thought.

"It was a trojan horse." Mayor Sorento tugged at the crisp white collar of his shirt as if he couldn't breathe. "He was ahead of his time when it came to these things."

"People were sent a link through an email and, if they clicked on it, a bug was loaded on their computer allowing hackers to trace their every click," Sheriff Ross said. "But it was more than that. The program allowed others to see emails as well as anything stored on the computer. It also allowed access to the microphone and camera. Johnny could access that at any time to eavesdrop on conversations."

"That's a total invasion of privacy." Lindsey shook her head, a tinge of outrage in her voice.

"It was," the sheriff continued. "Johnny convinced the mayor to let him prove it worked by attaching this trojan to an official email sent out by the county wishing residents Merry Christmas and encouraging them to click a link to donate to kids in need. If his plan worked, he wanted to eventually sell it to the federal government. He thought it could go far in helping them solve crimes."

Finn glanced around the group again. "Let me guess. You were all investors?"

"That's right." Mayor Sorento tugged on his collar again as regret filled his gaze. "It sounded like great technology to invest in. Johnny had promised us an amazing return on whatever we paid. It was almost too good to pass up."

"So, what happened?" Finn asked, not liking where this story was going.

"We had asked him to show us proof of concept for the project." Irma frowned, the worry in her gaze deepening. "And he did by sending that official county email with the trojan virus on it. We were impressed at first. However, somebody took that proof of concept a little too far and began to find dirt on all of us."

More details began to click in place.

"What happened next?" Lindsey asked.

Based on the look that they all gave each other, Finn wasn't sure he really wanted to know.

Because it most likely led to a chain of bad events . . . including Johnny's death and Lindsey's abduction.

CHAPTER FORTY-FIVE

LINDSEY COULDN'T BELIEVE what she was hearing. Couldn't believe that her parents would have been involved with something like this. But there was no denying the truth.

Something was going on here.

Something horrible.

"We all began getting threats to expose our darkest secrets." Sheriff Ross pushed his hand from his jaw to the back of his neck, tension threading through his gaze. "The person sending these threats would expose us if we didn't do a favor for them."

"I take it that someone threatened to expose your affair?" Lindsey asked, remembering Howie had mentioned it.

A shadow formed over his eyes. "That's correct. I had to let a couple of people go that I'd arrested in return for this person's silence. I had no idea what I had unleashed when I agreed to this project."

"This person also went after Maple's mom for stealing money," Lindsey said, as more facts clicked into place.

Mayor Sorento nodded. "I assumed that's what happened because blackmail and extortion began to spread outside this group to other people in town."

Lindsey turned to Fred. "You?"

His face fell into an expression of remorse. "I almost took my own life when my wife tried to leave me. It was . . . humiliating, not anything I wanted people to know about."

"Mrs. Whitley?" Lindsey continued.

She glanced away, clearly not liking the fact that her dignity was on the line. "This person threatened to expose my bank records. One of my husband's companies treated its employees poorly. They were severely underpaid. I disassociated myself with that business and tried to bury the connection. But someone found out I was still getting distributions from the company's profits."

Irma volunteered her secret without prodding. "I

told your parents when I wanted to buy the carriage house that my family had history with the place. I'd rented it for so many years, and it felt like home to me. I was afraid they would want to expand the inn and use my property there. So, I lied to them. As a result, they let me buy the carriage house. I'm not sure they would have if I hadn't made that emotional plea."

Finally, Lindsey's gaze fell on the mayor. "You might as well confess also."

He narrowed his eyes. "I had two sexual harassment suits against me. I paid off the women for their silence, but someone found out."

"And threatened to expose you . . ." That explained why he'd looked like he was keeping secrets earlier. Because he *was*. As was everyone here.

Mayor Sorento nodded slowly, regret in his gaze. "Exactly."

Lindsey let out a long breath as she processed everything. "And somehow someone found out that my parents were involved in the hit-and-run accident that took the lives of Ted and Janine."

A sick feeling gurgled in her stomach as she said the words aloud.

"That's right." The sheriff raised his chin, suddenly stoic. "We believe that your parents were talking about it when the microphone on the computer was accessed."

"Why didn't they just report it?" she asked.

"My guess is that they panicked," the sheriff said. "I'm sure their deaths were an accident. I have a feeling they were wrestling with what to do—and probably afraid that confessing might mean losing you."

The sick feeling in her gut churned harder. "Do you have any idea what someone asked them to do in order to keep silent?"

Lindsey held her breath, not sure she wanted to know what that answer was.

"Basically, they were supposed to be puppets." Irma wrung her hands together, and her expression was pinched with regret as she stood to the side of their circle. "They had to accept guests here who couldn't pay—give them priority over those who could. They had to turn a blind eye to some shady activities taking place on the beach at night. Basically, they had to do whatever this person said—or their secret would be revealed. They didn't tell me that directly. They only hinted that something was going on. I put the rest together."

"My best guess is that when they didn't comply, that's when you were abducted," Sheriff Ross said. "Your parents had to come up with fifty thousand dollars to get you back. I only know that they needed money because they asked me for a loan. They didn't tell me the exact reason for it. Either way, they didn't have that money—neither did I. The inn was in trouble, and they were barely able to keep it open as it was."

"Did they manage to come up with the funds?" Lindsey couldn't imagine how they would be able to do that.

"I let them have the cash." Mrs. Whitley offered a half eye roll as if she hated to admit any involvement. Her frantic fan waving paused for a moment. "By that time, we all assumed what was going on, though we never spoke of it. We couldn't because we didn't know who was behind it. I couldn't believe this person was willing to hurt an innocent child in order to get what he wanted. It made me sick to my stomach to think about."

"And you all thought Benjamin's father was the puppet master?" Lindsey asked. "In fact, he was probably lured away from the inn that night just to ensure he'd look guilty, wasn't he? He was set up from the start."

The cruelty of the person behind this continued to stun her.

"We honestly thought he was guilty at first. We thought maybe he'd overheard us talking at one of our meetings. His arrest was honest. But even after he died, the threats continued." Mayor Sorento frowned. "We were wrong."

"Did you ever suspect Johnny?" Finn asked. "He obviously had access to all the information."

"The thought crossed our minds, of course," Sheriff Ross stated. "But he had much more to gain from selling the program to the government than he could ever extort out of us."

Finn shook his head, appearing perplexed as he stared at everyone. "So, if Johnny wasn't behind everything, then who was?"

Everyone glanced at each other again, but no one seemed to have an answer to that question.

***

FINN'S MIND raced as he tried to figure out exactly what was going on here. Obviously, someone in this group had called everyone here and had a plan.

Whatever it was, Finn had a feeling there wouldn't be a happy ending.

"I say we get out of here." Sheriff Ross stepped back. "There's no reason for us to stick around. I know how it's going to end if we stay here."

"I agree." Mayor Sorento rolled his shoulders back, even though his unsteady gaze indicated he was afraid. "I don't like being a puppet."

"I, for one, am ready to leave." Mrs. Whitley raised her chin again as if daring someone to argue.

But no one did. They all began heading toward the door.

Finn wasn't sure everyone leaving was a good idea—not when someone here could be a killer. Someone here had most likely killed Johnny.

Before anyone reached the door, footsteps sounded above them.

The entire group froze.

Tension crept up Finn's spine.

Someone else was in this house.

He glanced up, wondering who it could possibly be. Who else might be involved?

Did Colin have some type of twisted connection to this? Maple?

He couldn't know for certain. He'd assumed someone in this circle was the culprit. Everyone seemed to have a motive.

Just then, a figure came down the staircase.

Finn sucked in a breath. "Howie . . ."

The man clucked his tongue as if he felt sorry for all of them.

"I'm the one who called you all here," he started, an amused tone to his voice and a new sparkle in his gaze. "And I suggest that none of you move."

The sheriff reached for his gun.

"I wouldn't do that if I were you," Howie murmured.

"Why not?" Sheriff Ross demanded.

"Trust me—you don't want to know."

The sheriff stepped toward the front door. "I'm not going to stick around any longer for this. I don't suggest any of you do either."

"While I was helping wire this place, I had enough time on my own to plant some explosives in the walls." Howie held up a detonator in his hand. "All I have to do is squeeze this and the whole place will go up in flames. Any questions?"

Everyone glanced at each other as if unsure how to proceed.

"That's what I thought." Howie reached the first floor and turned to address the group. "I'm so glad you could all make it. Sheriff, I need you to put your gun down and slide it across the floor to me."

The sheriff scowled. After a moment of contemplation, he let out a heavy sigh and did as Howie asked.

"Do the same with your other gun—the one you keep near your ankle," Howie continued.

The sheriff rolled his eyes but complied.

Howie kept one hand on the gadget and, with the other hand, he grabbed the sheriff's guns. Once he had one gun tucked into his waistband and the other in his free hand, he turned back to all of them.

"What are you doing, Howie?" Lindsey stared up at him, her voice trembling.

Finn felt sweat spreading across his forehead when he saw that gun. He knew how much damage it could do. He'd seen it firsthand on the battlefield.

"I'm finishing what should have been finished a long time ago," Howie announced. "Everybody in this town is simply pathetic. *Pathetic.*"

Finn bristled. The only reason Howie would have gone through all this trouble would be to teach them a lesson. What better lesson to teach than death?

He clenched his jaw so hard it ached. "You've already got everybody exactly where you want them. Why gather everyone here now?"

"Because power is nothing if you don't do something with it. And people in this room have abused their powers to no end. It's time they pay the price for doing that."

"Isn't that what you've been doing for the past fifteen or sixteen years?" Sheriff Ross nearly snarled as he said the words. "Punishing us?"

"I thought blackmailing you all would be enough, but I still see what you're all doing," Howie said. "I know all of you will have a price that can be paid for your soul. Whether it's money, love, power, help—everyone can be bought."

"What's your price?" Lindsey stared at Howie, a touch of defiance in her gaze.

Howie's smile drooped. "That's not important."

She was onto something—and Finn knew the answer to her question.

"It's revenge," Finn said. "Howie has done all of this to make it clear that he has the power to exact revenge over the most powerful people in this town." Everything began to click into place. "How did you disguise your voice on the phone, Dawson Smith?"

"I didn't have to try very hard." Howie strode across the room until he was in Finn's face. His cheeks reddened, and his actions appeared jerky with a mix of adrenaline and vengeance. "People hear what they expect to hear. They see what they expect to see. Don't they, Benjamin? Or should I say Finn Washburn?" he growled. "And don't act like you're any better than me. It wasn't so hard to convince you to come here under false pretenses, was it?"

"How did you even find me? How did you know I'm Benjamin's cousin?"

"When I found out Lindsey was coming back to renovate this place, I knew I needed a person to find the trunk before she did. Benjamin was my first choice. But he was unavailable. So I did the next best thing. I found someone who looked like Benjamin and knew all the details about his past. The fact you were a PI was icing on the cake, wouldn't you say? You were the perfect person for the job."

Finn kept his chin raised, not wanting to give Howie the upper hand in any way. "Lindsey already knows the truth about who I am. If you're trying to start trouble, you're too late."

"I'm not trying to start trouble. I *am* trouble." Howie's voice hardened. "You're all pawns in the game I'm playing. So, in case I haven't thanked you yet, I just wanted to say how much I appreciate you all showing up. But we don't have much time to chat and catch up. We need to get to work executing the game plan I've set up for everyone in the room."

Game plan?

Finn sucked in a breath.

If Howie had his way, none of them would get out of this alive, would they?

CHAPTER FORTY-SIX

MEMORIES DUG their talons into Lindsey's mind. At once, she was transported back in time.

The man hanging from the tree. Terror washing through her. Calling for Benjamin.

But before he could reach her, someone grabbed her. A bag covered her head. A prick stabbed her arm.

Everything went black.

Then she woke up.

In a dark space.

She was cold. Hungry. Scared.

So, so scared.

Everything around her spun, and she pulled her knees closer to her chest, desperate for warmth and comfort.

"You're awake." Someone shoved something into her hand. "You need to eat."

She startled. Did she recognize that voice? She didn't know.

"Where are my parents?" Lindsey blinked, trying to get her vision to clear.

"Just eat. You'll see them again soon. Maybe." The figure in front of her remained faceless and blurry.

But his voice . . . it sent chills through her.

He was so gruff, so angry.

Fear swelled in her blood.

Who was talking to her? Where was she? What had happened?

"I'm just going to make this easier on myself," the man growled as he loomed over her.

Lindsey tried to withdraw, to pull herself away. To scream. To do anything.

But she couldn't move. Walls surrounded her.

Rough walls. A cold floor.

Before she could do anything, she felt another prick.

But not before her vision cleared and she saw someone in front of her.

Lindsey snapped back to the present. She stared at Howie as he stood in front of them all, gun and detonator in hand. His voice had changed from the happy tone he'd used while rewiring her house.

Now she recognized it.

"You're the one who abducted me," she muttered to Howie.

How had she not seen this before? Why hadn't she sensed the danger around him?

But the memories had been repressed, blocked out.

Now they hit her at full force—speeding her pulse, tightening her lungs, accelerating the perspiration racing across her skin.

"You remember." Howie smirked as if he'd just been waiting for her to give him credit.

Lindsey's heart raced as panic tried to claim her. But she couldn't let that happen. She had to remain in control.

He'd get too much pleasure out of it otherwise.

"You're the one who hung Johnny on that tree," she said. "But I was never supposed to see you out there, and I must have. Or you were afraid that I did. That's why you grabbed me."

"Maybe."

"But you didn't know what to do with me," Lindsey continued. "So, you took me to an old hunting cabin in the woods and placed me in a closet there until you could figure it out—until you could use my abduction as leverage to get what you wanted from my parents."

"Go on." Satisfaction dripped from his voice.

"Once you had your money, you put me in the woods for the authorities to find and so you could wipe your hands of my abduction. It didn't matter at that point because Benjamin's father had been arrested and he died in jail within a week of being there. You made sure everyone thought he was responsible."

"I hadn't planned on him having a heart attack, but you have to admit the timing couldn't have worked out any better."

Lindsey narrowed her eyes at the absence of regret in his gaze. "You're sick. Absolutely sick."

"Johnny and I went to high school together," Howie explained. "No one else wanted to listen to him talk about computers, but I did. I could tell he was smart. I went into the computer shop one day, and I saw that familiar glimmer in his eyes. I knew he was up to something. I asked him about it and, after some persuasion, he told me about the program he was developing. I even got him to show me how it worked."

"But how did you find out everyone's secrets?" Finn asked.

"While I was doing some electrical work for him, I poked around on his computer. I began finding out information on everyone. The first group of people he had info on was his investors." Howie shrugged. "I went from there."

"Did you blackmail Johnny?" Mayor Sorento asked.

"I told him what he was doing was illegal and that I was going to go to the FBI. He panicked. I told him I'd remain silent if he gave me a copy of the program. He did. But, after a while, he got cold feet. He said he was going to go straight to the FBI and confess to his part in what I was doing. I couldn't let him do that. I had to make him an example of what would happen if you didn't play by my rules."

"So, his death was all part of your strategy?" Lindsey continued. "Part of your game?"

Howie smirked. "That's right. And you, my dear, were the star player. You will be again."

In one move, he grabbed her arm and jerked her toward him. The gun went to her temple as his other arm wrapped around her, the detonating device still clutched between his fingers.

Disgust rushed through Lindsey's veins, immediately followed by cold fear when she realized the position she was currently in. "What are you planning on doing with me?"

She glanced at Finn and saw his wide eyes and stiff muscles.

He was worried.

Truthfully, so was she. More than worried. She was scared out of her mind.

"This is what happens when you disobey me. I told you to leave. You didn't. It turns out that everyone here right now needs to be reminded again about what's at stake," Howie said. "So, we're going to re-create one of the historical moments that took place in this town. Everyone who lives here should be so proud." Sarcasm dripped from Howie's words.

Irma gasped as if she realized what was coming.

The sense of foreboding in Lindsey's gut made her lightheaded. She should realize the truth, but she couldn't bring herself to face it. "What does that mean?"

"It means that, in the old days, when people did something wrong, they were hung on the tree outside this inn. Tonight, we're going to re-create that, and you are going to be the criminal we all watch die."

Lindsey's lungs seemed to fill with cement until

she couldn't breathe as the implications of Howie's statement washed through her. Certainly, he wouldn't really hang her, would he?

But she knew the truth.

He would. He was going to hang her.

"I didn't do anything wrong." Her voice cracked as she said the words.

"You came back. You didn't get the hint when I told you to leave."

"Were you the one who threw the brick through the window?" Lindsey asked. "But what about Leo's fingerprint? How did it turn up on the paper?"

Howie glanced at the sheriff. "Do you want to tell her or should I?"

Sheriff Ross at least had the decency to hang his head. "I got another threat, with instructions about the fingerprint. But it wasn't real. None of it was."

Lindsey sucked in a breath as more shock coursed through her.

Howie turned back to her. "Now I need you to disappear—permanently. Maybe I should have done that the first time I had a chance, back when you were only twelve."

"This is senseless." Finn stepped closer, only stopping when Lindsey let out a gasp as Howie pushed the gun into her temple harder.

No matter how mad Lindsey was at Finn, something about his presence brought her comfort. He'd been protective of her even in his deception. She appreciated that security now.

But she wasn't even sure that Finn could save her . . . or that any of them could.

"Everyone here is going to witness your execution." Finn's voice sounded at a growl. "You're not going to get away with it."

"Nobody's going to admit what really happens here today, I have dirt I can spill on them." Howie's smirk widened. "There's always dirt. Always."

Lindsey had a feeling this was about more than just her and Howie. He got some type of delight in doing this. Maybe he was bored with his life in a small town, so this was what he'd chosen to do in order to pass his time. His gaze had seemed off tonight, like something wasn't quite right. She suspected he was taking more than one kind of drug—both of the legal and illegal sort.

"Everybody outside or I'm going to hit this button." Howie held up the detonator. "Or I'll shoot Lindsey. Whichever comes first."

"You don't have to hurt anyone." Finn seemed to plead with Howie with his gaze.

"If that's what I have to do, that's what I have to do. It's just another rule of the game."

Lindsey's gaze locked with Finn's for a moment. She saw the worry there, saw the protectiveness.

But Lindsey had no idea how this was going to play out.

She could only pray that it would end with everyone still alive.

FINN'S MIND raced as he was ushered outside with the rest of the group.

As soon as he stepped through the back door, he saw it.

A noose.

It had been hung from one of the massive branches extending from the oak tree.

Queasiness swept through him as he looked at it.

How could Howie be this sick? There was clearly something not right with the man. No one could deny that.

But Finn had to figure out how to get out of this situation—to get *Lindsey* out of this situation—without her being harmed.

With his gun still pressed into Lindsey, Howie

paced the perimeter of the space and began lighting some torches that had been set up. He'd left the detonator inside. Finn assumed it was no longer useful—not now that he had a noose.

The man had really thought everything through, hadn't he?

More acid gurgled inside Finn at the thought. He had to figure out a way to curtail this situation. One man should not have this much power to destroy others' lives.

Darkness hung around them, only offset by the glow of the torches. If Howie had wanted to re-create a moment from history, he'd succeeded.

That wasn't to mention the fact that no one else was around to see this. It was totally secluded out here, with only the bay and those being blackmailed as witnesses.

Finn needed to stall, he realized. At least until he could figure out a better plan. He had to buy some time.

"Why did you hire me to find that trunk?" Finn asked. "Why go through all that trouble?"

"As I said before, when I found out Lindsey was coming back, I needed to know what happened to it. If you need me to spell it out for you, it's because I needed to be sure no evidence could lead back to me." Howie paused by an old wooden chair that had been placed under the noose and began setting up a ladder beside it. "I stashed Lindsey away in the cabin and then came back to put Johnny in the trunk. I thought about leaving him hanging on the tree there for everyone to see, but after Lindsey messed up my plan, I had to improvise. She wasn't supposed to be out there."

"Benjamin was out there too," Lindsey said quietly.

"He didn't see my face. Besides, no one listened to him. He was just the caretaker's son."

Finn's jaw tightened. "So, you went through all the trouble of tracking me down, giving me a cover story, and setting up this whole scheme? Why leave the trunk with the body in it behind in the first place?"

"After I put Johnny into the trunk, I heard a noise inside the house. I must have somehow awakened Lindsey's parents. I panicked."

"So, you just left the trunk there?" Sheriff Ross asked.

"It was too heavy to run with, and I didn't have much time. Lindsey's parents must have found it and hidden it."

"Why would they hide it?" Lindsey's eyes pooled with emotion.

"My guess is because they were afraid they'd be accused of killing him," Irma said. "It was better to hide the body and pretend it never happened."

Howie scowled. "I had no idea what they did with the trunk, but I knew things had the potential of turning ugly if it was found all these years later. At one time, I tried to burn this place down to see if it was somewhere inside. But that didn't work."

"But even after we found the trunk, you kept going with this whole charade." Finn tried to make sense of this man's logic, but it was impossible.

Howie shrugged. "I had to rethink my strategy. Besides, holding leverage over people is fun. It brings me fulfillment. What can I say?"

"Why did you kill Daniel?" Fred's gaze burned into Howie. "What did he ever do to you?"

A shadow crossed Howie's gaze. "I was waiting in the woods, trying to figure out if I could get a tree to fall across the lane and trap everyone here. As I did that, Daniel came walking toward the inn and saw me."

"What happened next?" Sheriff Ross eyed Howie with contempt. "Why was he walking?"

"He thought the gate might be closed. He didn't

want to risk it, so he parked on the road and walked. Anyway . . ." Howie narrowed his eyes as if annoyed. "I tried to come up with a cover story, but he started asking all these questions about what I was doing, and he wouldn't back off. We got into a fight, and I hit him across the head with a branch. I didn't mean to kill him. But he shouldn't have gotten in my way."

Howie had totally lost it. There was no doubt about that.

This man would certainly carry through with his threats.

At once, an idea on how to stop him hit Finn, and his gaze met Howie's.

He prayed this would work.

He had no other ideas right now.

"You can't do this," Finn announced.

Howie let out a condescending snort. "Watch me."

Finn stepped closer, not ready to back down.

Please, let this work. Please.

"What about your own secrets?" he asked.

Howie startled, his gaze narrowing. "I don't know what you're talking about."

Finn locked his gaze with Howie's. "But I think you do."

CHAPTER FORTY-SEVEN

LINDSEY HELD her breath as she listened. Howie had stepped away slightly, but the gun was still aimed at her. Now she could turn her head and see everything happening—which could be a blessing and a curse.

What could Howie's secret be? How did Finn know about it?

"You're bluffing." Howie's voice contained a touch of apprehension as he stared coolly at Finn.

"Am I?" Finn said. "I am a private investigator."

Howie scowled. "What are you saying?"

"You told me about some of the stories your grandfather told you. Your family has a sordid history with this inn, don't they?"

Howie's cheeks turned red. "What about it?"

"In fact, your great grandfather was one of the people who died here, wasn't he? You gave me hints, almost like you were teasing me, wanting me to put things together. What I didn't realize is the lengths you'd go to carry out your twisted revenge."

Howie stared at Finn, not denying his words.

"Your father and grandfather made sure you knew about the atrocities that occurred here. They drilled it into you as a child. Didn't they?"

A sheen spread across Howie's skin as his voice became thinner. "You have no idea what it feels like to be on the other side of things. To not be an influential, prominent person in this town. To be treated as if you're worthless."

Lindsey could feel the dampness as the man pressed the gun into her.

"What happened to your great grandfather is horrible," Finn said. "But none of us here had anything to do with it."

"I can't let her bring this place back to life. The inn deserves to rot, just like this town left my great grandfather to rot."

"Hurting Lindsey won't undo what's already been done. You can end this." Finn stepped closer, his voice calm and even. "Right now. You don't have to do this to make your point."

"I *do* have to do this." Howie's words came out faster and faster. "My family passed down the stories. My great grandfather was accused of murdering one of his employees. He didn't even have the chance to defend himself. He never got a trial. He was arrested and hanged from the inn's oak tree as the townspeople watched."

Howie's vengeance had deep, deep roots.

And that was going to make this whole ordeal even harder.

"I'm sorry that happened." Finn edged closer. "But we weren't there. We didn't stain your family's reputation like that."

"It doesn't matter. You're just like them. If you'd been alive back then, you would have done the same thing to my family. That's the way it worked. People who weren't in the club didn't stand a chance. They were the ones accused—just so other people could feel better and sleep at night. It wasn't right."

"You don't have to continue this tradition," Finn leaned in, his voice earnest and impressively patient. "We can end that terrible practice now."

Howie stared at him a moment, almost as if contemplating his words. Then he shouted, "Enough talking! It's time to get this show on the road."

With that, he jerked Lindsey onto a chair beneath the noose.

Her blood went cold as she realized she had little power to stop the events that had been put into motion.

BAD THINGS HAPPEN *when good people do nothing.*

The thought wouldn't stop racing through Finn's mind.

Maybe no one in this circle was truly good. They were all flawed. They'd all made mistakes.

But who hadn't? Mistakes proved you were human.

Their mistakes shouldn't mean they were forced to live under the weight of guilt and shame.

Howie might have a gun, but that didn't mean he had all the power.

Because Finn wasn't going to stand here and do nothing.

He knew he'd royally messed things up with Lindsey. It was probably too late to make it right.

But he couldn't let this standoff end with her death.

As Lindsey stood on the chair, Howie began climbing the ladder behind her, gun still in hand.

Once she had that noose around her neck, it would be hard to go back, hard to save her.

That's why Finn needed to act now.

He prayed that God would guide each of his actions . . . or this plan could totally backfire.

CHAPTER FORTY-EIGHT

LINDSEY FELT the tremor rake through her as she stared at the rope swinging in front of her face.

Would that loop end up causing her death? Would a simple rope—something otherwise so harmless—kill her, strangling the breath from her lungs?

Her heart beat faster.

Maybe she could run.

But Howie would shoot her if she did.

Her mind continued to race.

Maybe she could swing her leg back and kick him.

But when he recovered, he'd still shoot her.

"Put it around your neck," Howie growled as he pointed the gun at her. "Now."

The people who'd died this way . . . they must have been terrified. Their deaths must have been so painful. What if they'd been innocent?

Like Lindsey was innocent.

Or was she? Did she deserve this after what happened to those people around Staunton? If she had only acted sooner, she might have saved some of them.

A cry caught in her throat as guilt flooded her.

"Put it around your neck," Howie repeated. "I don't know why you're wasting time. You're just putting off the inevitable and making it worse for yourself. If you don't do it now, I'm going to shoot someone here right now. I don't know who. But someone."

Gasps sounded around her. Mrs. Whitley let out a cry. Irma clung to Fred. The mayor crept back. The sheriff reached for a holstered gun that was no longer there.

Only Finn remained unmoving, his gaze fastened to the scene.

Lindsey reached for the rope, nausea pooling in her gut as she realized she had no other choice.

If she didn't do what Howie said, he would harm other people.

More blood would be on her hands.

Just as her fingers touched the prickly fibers, she heard a yell.

She looked over as Finn charged toward Howie.

Then the gun blasted, sending a bullet . . . somewhere.

FINN HAD KNOWN he couldn't waste any more time.

Without thinking, he'd rushed at Howie.

His shoulder caught the man in the stomach, and he tackled him to the ground.

But not before the gun had discharged.

Lindsey! What if the bullet had hit Lindsey?

His heart pounded harder at the thought.

Howie still held the gun. Finn had to get it from him or there could be other casualties. He desperately prayed that Lindsey wasn't one of them.

The two of them wrestled on the sandy ground filled with sprigs of grass. Just as Finn would pin Howie, Howie would flip on him. The man was stronger than Finn had given him credit for.

But Finn was going to have to be stronger.

Finn flipped the man once more. Still pressing

Howie's hand into the ground, he used his other fist to sock the man in the jaw.

Howie moaned and flinched.

As he did, Finn slammed the man's hand into the ground.

But Howie's grip held strong.

"I could use some help here!" Finn yelled over his shoulder.

Everyone was frozen with shock, he realized.

Just then, sirens sounded in the distance.

Sheriff Ross appeared beside him and kicked the gun from Howie's hand. The weapon tumbled over the grass out of reach.

As it did, the sheriff reached down and pulled Finn off Howie. He took the man by his shirt and jerked him to his feet.

"No more," the sheriff muttered. "No more."

Finn helped secure Howie's hands behind him, and he held him in place as he listened to the vehicles pulling up to the front of the inn.

Finn's gaze scanned everyone around him. He spotted Lindsey standing near Irma, the older woman's arm around her shoulder.

But she appeared to be okay.

The rest of the group also appeared unharmed. That bullet must have missed everyone.

Thank God!

His gaze connected with Lindsey, and she mouthed, "Thank you."

They would have time to talk later. Right now, the state police flooded the scene.

As Finn glanced up at the noose once more, the sickly feeling remained in his stomach.

That had been close.

Too close.

Was he hoping for too much to wish Lindsey might forgive him?

CHAPTER FORTY-NINE

LINDSEY DESPERATELY WANTED a moment alone with Finn.

But the past couple of hours had been overwhelming as everyone had been questioned, and the state police had swarmed the inside of the inn looking for evidence. Thankfully, Sheriff Ross had managed to dial Officer Williams' number on his cell phone. Williams had overheard enough of what was going on that he knew to come.

The good news was that they hadn't found any explosives between the walls. Howie had apparently been bluffing.

Irma had told Lindsey that she'd pleaded with her parents to do whatever was being asked of them so Lindsey would be returned. She'd tried to do everything in her power to get Lindsey back.

By the time the police dismissed Lindsey, it was well past midnight. Irma had already been sent home, as had Mayor Sorento, Fred, and Mrs. Whitley.

Apparently, Officer Williams still had questions for the sheriff.

Rightfully so, if the man had been abusing his power in order to cover up his secrets.

As Lindsey left the dining room—where she'd been interviewed—she searched for Finn.

Part of her wanted to be mad at the man.

But a bigger part of her realized he'd put his own life on the line to save hers. He'd acted selflessly. With honor. With love.

How could she hold what he'd done against him after that?

It would take some time to forget. But she knew she had to forgive.

Finally, Lindsey spotted Finn chatting with one of the officers in the kitchen. It appeared his questioning had wrapped up.

When he looked up and saw her, he paused. His eyes widened, and his breathing seemed to still for a moment.

He excused himself and crossed the room to meet her, stopping in front of her. He was close enough to touch her, and she almost thought he would.

But he held his arms at his side instead.

"How are you?" Finn asked.

"I'm alive." Lindsey's throat burned as she said the words. "Thank you for stepping in."

"Of course. I couldn't let him put that noose around you."

She glanced behind her and nodded toward the door leading into the hallway where the staff had stayed.

Without saying anything, Finn took her elbow and led her that way so they could talk in private. As they stood in front of each other, Lindsey's throat tightened. She hardly knew what to say. Yet there was so much she needed to get off her chest.

"I was angry when I realized the truth about who you really are," she started. "Yet, in another way, I can understand your deception. I still don't approve of it, however."

"I don't blame you for that."

"But you were willing to give up your life for me." A cry lodged in her throat. "I can't thank you enough for that."

Finn stepped closer and rubbed her arm. "I would do it all over again—tackling Howie, that is. Not deceiving you."

Lindsey stared up at him, her gaze probing his. "Why didn't you tell me the truth sooner?"

"I tried to. We kept getting interrupted. Part of me was relieved that I could delay telling you the truth. I didn't want to think about the divide it would cause or own up to the fact that I'd been lying. I dreaded seeing the disappointment in your eyes."

She remained silent another moment.

"It was always me you saw," he said softly. "I just had a different name. I really was in the military. I really do remember coming here. And when I kissed you . . . my feelings . . . they were real. The kiss was real."

She swallowed hard but didn't say anything.

"Some of the stories and details I remembered from Benjamin," Finn continued. "But I truly hated every minute I had to deceive you."

Lindsey nodded slowly as he waited for her to respond. Despite the lies, she felt like she really did know the real Finn.

"What about Benjamin?" she asked. "Is he okay?"

"Benjamin is on an island in the Caribbean. He's traveled the world and is perfectly content to be a nomad. He's totally off the grid right now and doesn't even have any social media. He says his mysteriousness gives him a leg up with the ladies."

A smile tugged at her lips. "That sounds like him. I'm glad he's happy."

"Me too."

As their gazes caught once more, Lindsey reached up and pulled Finn into a hug. Their bond was unmistakable, despite everything that had happened—or maybe because of it. She couldn't imagine anyone else helping her here at the inn . . . or making her toes curl like Finn did.

"Maybe we should have a redo," she murmured.

He stepped back and offered a warm grin. Unspoken promises—and hope—warmed his gaze.

"I'd like that. Lindsey, I'm Finn Washburn." He extended his hand. "I'm looking for a job, and I'd love to help you fix up this place."

She stared at his hand a moment before grinning. "I'm Lindsey Waters, and I've been looking for a good, reliable handyman. You think you're up for the job?"

He glanced around and shrugged. "This old place? How could I pass it up?"

"Once you look behind the walls, you might change your mind."

"It's true that you never know what you might find when you start tearing walls down. Those walls might have been covering up dirty little secrets. I believe in restoration."

She smiled. "So do I."

But Lindsey had to wonder if he was talking about this inn or their relationship.

Without any more hesitation, she accepted his handshake. "You're hired, Finn Washburn."

CHAPTER FIFTY

A COOL, early December breeze moved across the water until it reached Lindsey and brushed her hair back from her face. Darkness hung around her, but the stars sparkled overhead, seeming to promise good things for the future.

It was hard to believe she'd been working on this place for nearly three months.

In January, right after Christmas, Hidden Shores Inn would officially reopen for business.

Lindsey shoved down a trickle of nerves, choosing instead to embrace the excitement of this new opportunity. It would be a fresh start for her. She was using her degree in marketing to promote the place online, and they already had several bookings. She'd also hired staff to come alongside her—including two housekeepers and a cook.

It was a leap of faith, but she felt certain this was what she was supposed to do.

As she stood there, strong arms wrapped around her waist from behind. She grinned and leaned back into the embrace.

Into Finn's embrace.

He'd been around ever since this whole fiasco started, and he hadn't left her side. He'd been a great handyman, a trustworthy friend, and . . . more.

Lindsey had forgiven him for lying to her, and the two of them were now happier than Lindsey could have ever imagined or hoped.

In fact, she'd even met some of Finn's family, including Natalie. They'd come to the inn to visit and had helped with some preparations for the opening. They'd been a huge help and had made her feel included.

Lindsey had helped set up a fundraising page online to bring in money for Natalie's surgery. She'd used her marketing background to help spread the word.

And she'd succeeded. Natalie had the money she needed, and the surgery was scheduled in two weeks.

Meanwhile, Sheriff Ross had been pulled from the job when state authorities learned what he'd done. He was facing charges.

Howie was in jail awaiting trial.

The rest of the supper club group was facing their own consequences—both personally and professionally.

But, in other ways, what had happened had brought the town together and bonded them.

"We're going to redeem this inn," Finn murmured in her ear. "Our pasts don't define us. And the past won't define this place any longer."

"I couldn't agree more." As Lindsey looked out over the water, her breath halted as something caught her eye. "Do you see that?"

"See what?"

She pointed at the shoreline, her heart pounding in her ears. "Bioluminescence."

"What?"

"It's what Benjamin and I sneaked out here to see that night . . . the night I was abducted. It's actually algae that glows in the water. It's rare to see around here. I never thought I'd get to see it twice in my lifetime."

"That's . . . amazing. Almost magical."

She turned in his arms so she was half facing

Finn and half facing the water. "I think so too."

He leaned forward and kissed her cheek.

Warmth filled her as he did. "I'm glad God brought you here, Finn—however strange those circumstances might have been."

A soft smile lit his face. "Me too. I'm really glad that He could take a twisted situation and turn it around for good."

"He has a way of doing that . . ."

They exchanged a smile before Finn reached down and pressed his lips against hers.

It was one of many kisses they'd shared since they'd officially become a couple.

Lindsey rubbed her fingers together and felt the engagement ring there.

The kiss was one of many more to come in the future.

Even better—the ring had a small skeleton key engraved on the inside of the band, promising Lindsey that Finn would always treasure having the key to her heart.

If you enjoyed this book, please consider leaving a review.

ALSO BY CHRISTY BARRITT:

Edge of Peril

When evil descends like fog on a mountain community, no one feels safe. After hearing about a string of murders in a Smoky Mountain town, journalist Harper Jennings realizes a startling truth. She knows who may be responsible—the same person who tried to kill her three years ago. Now Harper must convince the cops to believe her before the killer strikes again. Sheriff Luke Wilder returned to his hometown, determined to keep the promise he made to his dying father. The sleepy tourist area with a tragic past hadn't seen a murder in decades—until now. Keeping the community safe seems impossible as darkness edges closer, threatening to consume everything in its path. As The Watcher grows desperate, Harper and Luke must work together in order to defeat him. But the peril around them escalates, making it clear the killer will stop at nothing to get what he wants.

Margin of Error

Some secrets have deadly consequences. Brynlee Parker thought her biggest challenge would be hiking to Dead Man's Bluff and fulfilling her dad's last wishes. She never thought she'd witness two men being viciously murdered while on a mountainous trail. Even worse, the deadly predator is now hunting her. Boone Wilder wants nothing to do with Dead Man's Bluff, not after his wife died there. But he can't seem to mind his own business when a mysterious out-of-towner burst into his camp store in a frenzied panic. Something—or someone—deadly is out there. The killer's hunger for blood seems to be growing at a brutal pace. Can Brynlee and Boone figure out who's behind these murders? Or will the hurts and secrets from their past not allow for even a margin of error?

Brink of Danger

Ansley Wilder has always lived life on the wild side, using thrills to numb the pain from her past and escape her mistakes. But a near-death experience two years ago changed everything. When another incident nearly claims her life, she turns her thrill-seeking ways into a fight for survival. Ryan Philips left Fog Lake to chase adventure far from home. Now he's returned as the new fire chief in town, but the slower paced life he seeks is nowhere to be found. Not only is a wildfire blazing out of control, but a malicious killer known as "The Woodsman" is enacting crimes that appear accidental. Plus, there seems to be a strange connection with these incidents and his best friend's little sister, Ansley Wilder. As a killer watches their every move and the forest fire threatens to destroy their scenic town, both Ryan and Ansley hover on the brink of danger. One wrong move could send them tumbling over the edge . . . permanently.

Line of Duty

Jaxon Wilder didn't plan on returning home to Fog Lake, Tennessee, following his tour of duty in Iraq. But after a gut-wrenching failure during his stint in the Army, he now faces a new challenge: his family. Abby Brennan always did her best to be the good girl and to live by the rules. When a wrong decision changes her entire life, she tries to hide from the world. However, a madman known as the Executioner is determined to find her and enact his own brand of justice. When Jaxon and Abby are thrown together in the killer's crosshairs, they're forced to depend on one another to survive. Will Jaxon's sense of duty be enough to help keep Abby safe? Or will deadly secrets lead to the penalty of death?

ABOUT THE AUTHOR

USA Today has called Christy Barritt's books "scary, funny, passionate, and quirky."

Christy writes both mystery and romantic suspense novels that are clean with underlying messages of faith. Her books have won the Daphne du Maurier Award for Excellence in Suspense and Mystery, have been twice nominated for the Romantic Times Reviewers' Choice Award, and have finaled for both a Carol Award and Foreword Magazine's Book of the Year.

She is married to her Prince Charming, a man who thinks she's hilarious—but only when she's not trying to be. Christy is a self-proclaimed klutz, an avid music lover who's known for spontaneously bursting into song, and a road trip aficionado.

When she's not working or spending time with her family, she enjoys singing, playing the guitar, and exploring small, unsuspecting towns where people have no idea how accident-prone she is.

Find Christy online at:
www.christybarritt.com
www.facebook.com/christybarritt
www.twitter.com/cbarritt

Sign up for Christy's newsletter to get information on all of her latest releases here: www.christybarritt.com/newsletter-sign-up/

If you enjoyed this book, please consider leaving a review.

Made in the USA
Columbia, SC
20 October 2021

47557843R00250